"Hey Pig, Keep the Slop. I'm Going Home!"

A Journey

By

Brad Gamble

BOOK WRITING
PIONEER

Table of Contents

Introduction

Good day! What you hold in your hands has been on my heart for years, ever since I came to the end of my rope, and God met me there. As a workaholic skirting at the edge of divorce, Jesus met me where I was and walked with me through the tough work of restoring my life to what He desired and designed. This book is the story of that journey of restoration. Do you find yourself at your wit's end, trapped by past decisions, repeating an endless cycle that seems to keep leading you further off course from where you thought or wanted to be? I'm here to tell you that there is hope. Today is the first day of the rest of your life. Our futures are not written in stone, so take heart! I'm living proof!

A number of years after this journey began for me, I was called into recovery ministry and was amazed at the language that the steps layout for anyone interested in walking them. Here was the experience I'd lived but hadn't known how to put into words. Here were practical steps that *anyone* could embark on to meet our Heavenly Father and to experience the freedom He intends for us.

I say anyone because the 12 steps of AA (Alcoholics Anonymous), NA (Narcotics Anonymous), and CA (Cocaine

Anon…) too long have been set aside, dismissed as something for *those people*: addicts. If the 12 steps are for *those people*, then I guess I'm one of them, although I have not struggled with a chemical addiction. How can that be? At the center of addiction is a desire to escape or deal with an issue in our lives with the wrong solution. My solution was to work or bury myself in it specifically and expect the rewards (money) to fill the hole I felt in my life. Different solution from drinking or drugs but not so different when you look at the heart of the desire, so I guess I'm an addict too! How about you? Ever tried to escape or use a substitute as a solution?

Did you know that the 12 steps of AA, which have been adopted by all the other 12-step movements, were not created by the founders of AA? Granted, they took the time to lay them out in an understandable format, but they didn't create or come up with them. The twelve steps are actually all Biblical principles drawn from the Word of God. As such, they are meant for *everyone;* they are a life-changing path for all to follow. That's why I hope you will join me in this journey as we look at the Bible and explore what it has to say about them. We'll look at the written steps themselves to identify the issues because they do a masterful job of boiling them down so they're easy to understand. Then, we'll dig into the Word to see what our 12-step forefathers were trying to get at specifically.

If you don't believe in God or don't know what to believe, let me say that that's alright! You are welcome here, just as you are. Explore with me, and come to your own understanding in your own time. I believe that is what God wants for all of us. These next pages are meant to be a journey that we get to travel together. While it will require honesty and a lot of work, I believe that it's going to be both a fun time and a time of amazing growth!

So, with that being said, let's get to 'er!

Chapter 1
I Got This?

To begin our journey, we're going to start with step one. That makes sense, right? Starting at the beginning? :) So, what's step one? In AA literature, step one reads:

"We admitted we were powerless over alcohol - that our lives had become unmanageable." [1]

Now remember, this is the Alcoholics Anonymous step one, and so it refers to alcohol, but as we read the steps, I encourage you to substitute the word "alcohol" for whatever seems to have control in your life. This may be drugs, pornography, anger, food, co-dependency, money, sex, you name it. The issues may differ, but the steps are the same.

So what is this step getting at exactly? Well, I always find it easier to understand something if I can relate it to a story, to something concrete. So, we're going to look at a story in the Bible. It is a story about a son who runs away and squanders his inheritance. Hopefully, it will give us something practical to dig our teeth into in order to help us understand this step.

Do you know the story I'm referring to? It's about the prodigal or lost son and is found in the Gospel of Luke, chapter 15, verses 11 to 32. Let's read the story to get an overview of what message it has to convey, and then we'll look specifically at the first few verses and how they relate to step one and our lives.

"Jesus continued: "There was a man who had two sons. The younger one said to his father, 'Father, give me my share of the estate.' So, he divided his property between them. "Not long after that, the younger son got together all he had, set off for a distant country and there squandered his wealth in wild living. After he had spent everything, there was a severe famine in that whole country, and he began to be in need. So he went and hired himself out to a citizen of that country, who sent him to his fields to feed pigs. He longed to fill his stomach with the pods that the pigs were eating, but no one gave him anything. "When he came to his senses, he said, 'How many of my father's hired servants have food to spare, and here I am starving to death! I will set out and go back to my father and say to him: Father, I have sinned against heaven and against you. I am no longer worthy to be called your son; make me like one of your hired servants.' So he got up and went to his father. "But while he was still a long way off, his father saw him and was filled with compassion for him; he ran to his son, threw his arms around him, and kissed him. "The son said to him, 'Father, I have sinned against heaven and against you. I am no longer worthy to be called your son.' "But the father said to his servants, 'Quick! Bring the best robe and put it on him. Put a ring on his finger and sandals on his feet. Bring the fattened calf and kill it. Let's have a feast and

celebrate. For this son of mine was dead and is alive again; he was lost and is found.' So they began to celebrate. "Meanwhile, the older son was in the field. When he came near the house, he heard music and dancing. So he called one of the servants and asked him what was going on. 'Your brother has come,' he replied, 'and your father has killed the fattened calf because he has him back safe and sound.' "The older brother became angry and refused to go in. So his father went out and pleaded with him. But he answered his father, 'Look! All these years, I've been slaving for you and never disobeyed your orders. Yet you never gave me even a young goat so I could celebrate with my friends. But when this son of yours who has squandered your property with prostitutes comes home, you kill the fattened calf for him!' " 'My son,' the father said, 'you are always with me, and everything I have is yours. But we had to celebrate and be glad because this brother of yours was dead and is alive again; he was lost and is found.' " Luke 15:11-32 NIV

Kind of a feel-good story where things work out in the end, eh? A good example of grace extended and restoration, don't you think?

So, what was step one again? *"We admitted we were* <u>*powerless*</u> *over alcohol—that our lives had become* <u>*unmanageable."*</u> Two words jump out: powerless and unmanageable. Strong words that give you that sinking feeling when you personalize them. So, how do they relate to the story of the prodigal son?

Well, let's recount this story again. It starts out with a man and his two sons. The younger son, we see, is impetuous and, frankly, pretty selfish. He decides he knows best and wants to live life his way. Can you relate, BTW? Ever believe you had it all figured out? :) The son goes to his father and demands what would be his after his father dies *before* he dies! Can you imagine a son saying that to his father? "Hey, Dad, I'm gonna get your stuff when you die, so can I rather have it now?" I know what my answer would've been! But the father in this story gives in to his son's demands and gives him his inheritance. It's not until later in the story that we see why.

So the son, having gotten his money, moves far away and basically blows everything on a party life. Can you relate? :) About the time his money is running out, a famine strikes the land and he's forced to work for a pagan farmer, tending his pigs. This part of the story shows us how far the son has fallen. Pigs are considered unclean animals in Jewish tradition and should be avoided, as should non-Jewish people. And yet, the son is so desperate that he finds himself becoming "unclean" as well. He's forced to be around them and is so hungry that he looks longingly at the food being given to these unclean animals. Here's the part of the story I want us to look at.

How did the son get there? Do you think this was where he saw his plan leading him when he asked his father for his portion of the family estate? Thinking back on our own lives, when things did not turn out as we'd hoped, was that the plan from the beginning? Are we a bunch of masochists determined to chart a course to our own destruction? Of course not. We always start out with the best of intentions, don't we? So it was with the prodigal son. I'm sure he had great plans when he set out—plans to make a worth-living life for himself, seeking a meaningful relationship, a loving family, and a successful career. He may have gone about it the wrong way, starting out demanding his inheritance, but I'd be willing to bet that he intended for his life to be a good one.

So what went wrong? Why do you think things went sideways? The story tells us that he wasted his money on wine, women, and music. Was he blind to the bank statements coming in saying that his account was steadily going down? Why wouldn't he have set aside some of his funds and invested them so he'd have a secure future? Wouldn't that have made sense to him? Wouldn't that make sense to us?

What is it that the Apostle Paul says in Romans chapter 7?

"The trouble is with me, for I am all too human, a slave to sin. I don't really understand myself, for I want to do what is right, but I don't do it. Instead, I do what I hate." Romans 7:14-15, NLT

Paul shares the insight with us that, as fallen beings, we don't have complete control over ourselves and our inner desires. He says we are slaves to sin. There is something that has control or power over us. The prodigal son thought he had control, didn't he? He thought he was the master of his own destiny. He was all that and a bag of chips. But we see the truth through this story, don't we? He wasn't really in control. If he was, why would he have allowed himself to get into such a desperate situation? Why didn't he take the appropriate steps early to ensure he'd have the life he planned?

Self-deception is a powerful force. We're going to look at it more in-depth in a few chapters, but for now, we can quickly look at the story so far and see that the son must have been living under its influence. He believed fully in his own abilities, believing the lie that he had things under control. What else could possibly explain his actions—or, more to the point, his inaction in changing his situation?

We're told in the story twice that the son wasted his money on women, first in wild living and, more specifically, later by his brother, on prostitutes. Do you think that was his intention when he left home? No, he probably had plans to make a good life for himself. He dreamed of ultimately settling down, having a family, and being a successful businessman. So what's this whole prostitute business about? Do you think he figured that was a good place to start? To find a long-lasting relationship to build into? Doubtful right?

I suspect he thought he'd "enjoy life" for a while. He was young. There was a lot of time to settle down, find a good woman, and build a life together. What could having a night of "fun" before that possibly hurt? One won't hurt, right? Ever heard and believed that before? Hard to stop there, isn't it? We get a taste, and it tastes good. Besides, we're in control, and we can handle it. We can stop anytime. So we have a second taste, and things seem to continue alright, don't they? Life goes on. Then a third time, fourth, fifth. I think that's what happened with the prodigal son. He got caught up in his new life of fun, truly believing he was in charge and that he could continue with his plans the next day. Remember, self-deception is a powerful thing.

I Got This?

We're told that the son wasted his money on prostitutes and wild living. What do you think the wild living part entailed? Perhaps some partying? Some drinking? Some eating? How about some newfound "friends" who always seem to appear when there's money in the air? Do we think the prodigal son planned to spend all his money on those things? I doubt it, but his bank account continued to drain.

Here's a question: Why do you think we seem to believe that we can give up control in one area of our life and still maintain it in others, that it won't impact them? If we look at the step we read earlier, we're powerless over (whatever our particular drug of choice is). Why do you think that lack of control in one area of our life won't affect our ability to manage other aspects of our lives? Our relationships, our jobs, our health—why do we believe these domains remain unaffected? The son in this story seemed to hold just such a belief that he could dabble with prostitutes and not experience a similar lapse in judgement in other areas of his life. And yet, we see that his indiscretions led to a complete downfall, we're told that he squandered his wealth, spending everything.

If we look back at the details of the story, we start to get some answers. The prodigal son starts down a different path, the same path I hope all of us realize we need to be on. This is the crux of the matter for step one. Verse 17 tells us:

"When he finally came to his senses, he said to himself, 'At home, even the hired servants have food enough to spare, and here I am!" dying of hunger."

It says he "came to his senses." What does that mean? Up until now, in the story, I think we'd agree that the son's decisions and actions have not made much sense. They certainly have not been leading to his prosperity and future security, have they? So, his coming to his senses can be seen as realizing and understanding that he has not been making wise decisions. The second part of his statement highlights the depth of his newfound realization. He recognizes that his actions have led him to a dead end. *"Here I am..."* You can hear the depth of his sorrow, the recognition of how far he's fallen.

I wonder how many of us have faced a similar moment. Looking around, albeit a bit unbelievingly, at our surroundings and wondering, "How on earth did I get here?" How did I not see this coming?" Maybe that's been sitting in a jail cell, or in a hotel room rented by the hour, or sitting in an empty house reading a "Dear John or Jane" letter. Whatever the case, we suddenly come to our senses and see the truth of our situation and actions. We've been deceiving ourselves, claiming to have control. If we really had control, why would we ever have let it come to this?

Paul shares our realization with his confession that *"the trouble is with me, for I am all too human, a slave to sin."* We don't have control; control is an illusion. We *are* powerless over our addictions. That is a simple truth I hope we grasp.

In this story of the prodigal son, we see the results of his powerlessness. His life has become unmanageable. While engaging in his addiction, he tried to control his own life but failed to manage his affairs in a way that would allow him to continue. By his own admission, he is *"dying of hunger!"* The only thing he has managed to do is put his life in jeopardy! What do we do with managers who don't manage things well? We fire them! We take away their ability to make decisions and give it to someone who can.

Well, this story is no different. The prodigal son finally comes to terms with the fact that he is not in control and is faced with a choice. When we recognize that we are not really in control and are powerless over our addiction, we are faced with a similar choice. We can continue to deceive ourselves, believing we can somehow regain control, or we can recognize that we're not up to the task. Perhaps we are truly powerless and should start looking for another solution. As we read in the story, the prodigal son decides to turn to his father for a solution, and we'll explore that further in the coming chapters.

Right now, I hope we can come to recognize that we are all broken. We all struggle with something. As Christians, we lump it all into one term: sin. Scripture tells us:

"for all have sinned and fall short of the glory of God" ~Romans 3:23.

We're not perfect, and we don't live in a perfect world. For those who do not share my walk of faith, call it what you want. Our particular sin or struggle looks different for each person. It could be selfishness, lust, or a chemical dependency—it doesn't matter. Whatever it is, when we engage in it and believe that we are in control, it slowly grows and infects all aspects of our lives. Ultimately, our lives become unmanageable, and that sucks. :(

However, there *is* a light at the end of the tunnel. If you've been following along so far and recognized that life with us at the helm is not the best, then you've taken the first step. You've flicked the switch and sent power to that light. Over the rest of this journey, we'll walk down that tunnel, taking each step as it comes. We'll be walking side by side, supporting each other along the way, and I think that's pretty exciting! So congratulations—you may be powerless now, but I believe you're more secure than you've ever been. This journey is not meant to be a blind leap of faith, so to speak; let's dig into the following chapters. Like the prodigal son, start looking for another solution to your insanity!

Prayer

Heavenly Father please help us to recognize that we do not and cannot control everything in our lives. Help us to recognize where we are powerless over our addiction(s) and yet also see that this admission is the first step towards the restored and full life You desire for us. Fill us with hope of a better future! Thank You, Lord. Amen.

Questions

1. What am I powerless over and has made life unmanageable? What is the one thing I struggle with that has spilled over and

affected all areas of my life?

2. How have I deceived myself in the past? What role has self-deception played in my life?

3. Does the idea of being powerless frighten me? Why?

Chapter 2
You Know the Way...

So you're ready for something different in life? Being willing to look at ourselves honestly is a huge first step. Having taken it, we're now ready to look at the second step in our journey. So, what is that second step? If we turn to 12 step literature, the second step is defined as:

"We came to believe that a power greater than ourselves could restore us to sanity."

Before we move forward into this new step however, I want to look again at where we began. Every journey begins with a first step, so let's recall what it was and make sure that we're on firm footing before venturing on.

Last chapter we looked at the story of the prodigal son. If you recall, he'd demanded his own way, his share of the family fortune, and ran off to live life. Well, things didn't go that well for him, did they? We read that he ended up wasting everything on wine, women and music and had to resort to making a living feeding pigs for a local farmer. If you remember, life got so bad that he was dying of starvation. He was looking hungrily at what he was feeding the pigs! Just a little off the mark from his initial plan right?

As the first step in our journey, we looked at the realization that we are powerless over our addictions, our vices, and our human nature—call it what you will. We examined Paul's confession, *"I don't really understand myself, for I want to do what is right, but I don't do it. Instead, I do what I hate."* Is that thinking familiar to you? We asked ourselves if this is true in our own lives. Do we do what we don't want to and fail to do what we want to? Are we like the prodigal son, suddenly looking around us and wondering how on earth we got here? *This isn't where I thought I'd be.* We never plan to go where some of our choices take us, believing we are in control. But when we look at the evidence, that control seems to be a mist, an illusion. When we truly look at our story, we recognize that we're in the same boat as the prodigal son—we're just as powerless.

Now, that seems to be pretty disheartening. But remember, although we've come to recognize that we're powerless, we're actually more secure than ever because of that realization. We're now ready to take the second step to restoration.

"We came to believe that a power greater than ourselves could restore us to sanity."

Believe—what does that mean? According to the dictionary, it is *"to think that something is true, correct or real.[2]"* So what is it that this step is telling us we must believe? That a power greater than ourselves can restore us to sanity. A power greater than ourselves—

what is at the heart of that? I don't want to get into what the particular power is right now, just what this "power" boils down to in its simplest form. 12-step literature is written in such a way that this power can be whatever you believe it to be, a power of your own understanding. When we look at the statement, we see that at this particular moment, it doesn't matter what the power is, but where it is. "A power greater than ourselves". Five simple words that call us to step *outside* ourselves.

Remember that step one was us realizing that we are powerless. So, it makes sense that we need to look outside ourselves for a solution. We've come to realize that on our own, in our own broken power, we're struck. So where can we turn? Outside, to something *greater* than ourselves. That's a very important piece. We can turn to someone else, someone who suffers the same condition as us—namely, being human, but how far will that get us? About as far as our own power was taking us. This second step is all about believing that there can be a solution and that it is found in something greater than ourselves.

With that, let's return to the story of the prodigal son and see what it has to tell us. As I indicated before, we are going to look at the 12 steps and their Biblical foundations. The 12 steps were not conceived by the AA movement, they simply wrote down in an easy-to-understand format, Biblical principles for living. That is why we're looking to the Bible for more insight as we go through these steps and also why I encourage you to dig into the Bible. I guarantee you'll be amazed at what you find in it! Whether you believe it is the word of God or not, the wisdom to be found there is life-changing.

So, on with the story. Beginning in Luke, chapter 15, verse 17, we'll pick up where we ended off.

"When he finally came to his senses, he said to himself, 'At home, even the hired servants have food enough to spare, and here I am dying of hunger! I will go home to my father and say, 'Father, I have sinned against both heaven and you, and I am no longer worthy of being called your son. Please take me on as a hired servant." So he returned home to his father." vs 17-20a

The first verse is what we looked at in the last chapter. The son came to the realization that he was not where he had planned to be. Instead, he was exactly where he'd planned not to be, and he'd been powerless to prevent it. The second part of this verse is what I want us to explore now. The prodigal son recognized that his father's hired servants were better off than he was. He realized that his father was capable of taking care of others better than the son was able to take care of himself. Not only do we see the proverbial light coming on in the son's mind, but we also witness the solution presenting itself to him. You can almost hear the son talking to himself, can't you? (Or maybe I'm just personalizing this too much, putting myself in his shoes because they fit so well.) I see him standing amongst the pigs, ankle-deep in the mud, and hear him saying:

"Man, life here sure sucks. I don't understand what happened. One moment, I was having fun, and the next, I'm stuck here with these dirty animals. And they're eating better than I am! What's up

with that? How did I get here?"

...You know, when I think about it, even the servants back home have it better than this. Man, I'm hungry! I mean, Dad makes sure they have food on their table, doesn't he? But I really blew it, didn't I? Some son I turned out to be. ...Hey pig, you gonna eat all that?"

...Hmmm, maybe I could go home and work for Dad? He takes care of the servants, perhaps I should go join them? Yes! That's what I'll do. I'll go home as a servant, not as a son. Dad will help me like he does the others. Hey, pig, keep the slop, I'm going home!"

Now, in the rest of the story, we see that the sons' belief was justified. His father does look after him, providing a solution. But we'll look at that more closely in the coming chapters. So, the son recognizes his powerlessness and comes to believe that a solution outside himself exists, namely his father. He believes that he can get off this path of insanity that he's found himself on and regain some perspective and direction by looking to his Dad.

So what about us? We've considered our own lives and recognized that we don't really have the control we think we have. Can we be restored like the son in this story? What does that look like for us? Remember, the second step is coming to believe that a power greater than ourselves can restore us to sanity. What do you believe? Do you think that a power greater than yourself can help you? What does that power look like? How can it or He help you?

Earlier, I said I didn't want to look at the specifics of the higher power at that point. We just needed to recognize that we must look outside ourselves if we're going to find a solution. I believe we've done that. We've come to recognize that left on our own, we, by nature, screw it up. Therefore, the solution must lie outside ourselves. It has been my experience in my life that the higher power that has brought clarity to my insanity is God, namely Jesus Christ. I would like to tell you why I came to believe this, however and a bit of what the Bible has to say about Jesus. I'd like to look at a promise that God has made to us, and then I'll leave it in your hands to do with as you wish.

Ever gone to a professional sporting event or watched one on TV? Ever seen a banner there with a scripture reference? There is one most common reference we see at these events—"John 3:16". Why do you think that is such a popular quote? Because it sums up the promise of God. It reads:

"For God so loved the world that he gave his one and only Son, that whoever believes in him shall not perish but have eternal life." ~ John 3:16 NIV.

Ever heard that one before? Like I said, pretty popular, right? What does it tell us about God? It tells us a bit about his heart. How about our value? *"For God so loved the world..."*. How much does He love us? This passage tells us that he loves us enough to give up His own son. How many of us would give up our child for someone? God did. That's how much He loves us. It sounds like maybe someone you could trust to have your best interest at heart and lead you better than yourself.

Why did He give up His Son for us? The passage says it was so that we would not perish. Perish —immediately; the mind jumps to death, doesn't it? A ship sinks, or a plane crashes with all on board perishing. This passage does make that connection; God does not want us to die. But perish can also mean to spoil or deteriorate.

I've spent some time working in a commercial kitchen and have learned a lot about "perishables." Did you know that contrary to popular belief, putting spoiled milk back in the fridge does not make it better by the next day?

God does not want our lives to perish, spoil, or deteriorate either. He came *"that they may have life, and that they might have it more abundantly." John 10:10, KJV* scripture says. So we can look to this passage as a promise as well that He wants the best for us. He wants to guide us to better living, better decisions. He is the power greater than ourselves which can restore us to sanity. Will life be "happily ever after" with God at the helm? No, we don't live in fairytale land; we live in the world, the fallen world. Jesus Himself promises us that there will be struggles and strife. But, as we've learned, on our own, we're powerless and end up where we don't want to be—nowhere near where we'd planned! We've been exploring that any solution must come from outside ourselves. So, who better to look to than the One who loves you so much that He gave up His own Son for you? Who better to turn to than the One who wants to help you live life better—not to perish but to have life and have it abundantly?

So what are we to do? John tells us—believe! That's the only condition within this passage. Whoever believes in Him, whoever believes that Jesus gave up His life for us, whoever believes that God loves us so much that He would give up everything for us, will not perish but have eternal life! Belief—that's our second step. It's how this journey of restoration we're on gains traction. Believe not in our own power but in a power greater than ourselves!

The prodigal son came to his senses, we're told, and believed that his father could and would help him. We're faced with a similar decision. Are we going to believe in our Heavenly Father's promise, allow it to shape our lives, and lead us on a journey of restoration? Or are we going to continue relying on our own strength, following our own path, and reap the consequences that come with that?

I've made my decision, and I'm here to tell you that in my experience, God is faithful and trustworthy to keep His promises. Life has taken a markedly upward turn since I chose to believe in Jesus as the power greater than myself that can restore me to sanity. So again, I ask you: what do you believe? Just a question to ponder as we continue our journey together.

Prayer

Heavenly Father, You know that we are powerless over our addiction(s), and that's frightening. Please help us understand that our solution must come from outside and that You want the best for us. Help us to shed our fear and believe that You can restore us to sanity. Amen.

Questions

1. Am I at the end of my rope and willing to try something different? Do I see that a solution must come from outside myself because operating in my own strength is what got me here?

2. Am I ready to take God at His word, to believe His promise that He wants the best for me?

3. Do I believe that God can lead me on a path that can restore sanity to my life?

Chapter 3
You Take the Reins!

Welcome to the third step on our journey. It's been a bit of a voyage to get here, hasn't it? We've covered a lot of ground already and have had to look at ourselves in a new light.

Now, we're about to embark on step 3:

"We made a decision to turn our will and our lives over to the care of God as we understood Him."

We've been looking at the story of a particular son in the Bible. Do you remember his name? Yes, a bit of a trick question; that wasn't really fair. All we see him referred to as is the "prodigal son." Ever wonder why? Perhaps it's so we can identify with him more easily by putting our name in his place. Just a thought. So we've been looking at this story of the prodigal son, <u>Brad.</u> We've seen how he thought he knew best and really just got himself into a lot of trouble, didn't he? He took his inheritance and blew it on wild living far from home, ending up starving and feeding pigs for a living. We've explored how he finally recognized that it was his decisions that led him where he was and that he couldn't trust himself to make the big decisions. He always seemed to make the wrong ones, didn't he? He was powerless when it came to looking after his best interests. His vices or addictions or sins, whatever you want to call them, always seemed to gain the upper hand.

We've been looking at our own lives, too. As much as we hate to admit it, we have a lot in common with Brad, the prodigal son, don't we? Looking back throughout our lives, we can trace the detours we've taken off our best path to when we've decided to grab the wheel. (And I've always considered myself a good driver. Hmm.) We're all powerless and can relate to Paul's words, "*I want to do what is right, but I don't do it. Instead, I do what I hate.*" can't we?

Lastly, we looked at the part of the story where Brad began to believe that any solution to his problems must come from outside himself. He believed that his father could and would help him, didn't he? And we looked at the same thing in our own lives. We began to understand that the solution to our own powerlessness could be and is found in a higher power than ourselves. A higher power that we've named as God—Jesus Christ. It is through Him that we can look for the solution and be restored to sanity.

So that's where we're picking up the story from. Remember where the story of the prodigal son is found? (Lk 15:11-31). By the end of this journey, whenever you hear someone refer to this story, "Luke 15:11-31" will flash through your brain! I say that with humor, but it is actually good for us to know where to find things in

Scripture because it allows us to look to His Word for wisdom quickly. Whether you believe it's the Word of God or not doesn't matter. The wisdom to be found in the Bible, as it draws on thousands of years worth of life experience, is a resource you don't want to ignore.

So starting at Luke chapter 15, verse 18, we read:

"I will set out and go back to my father and say to him: Father, I have sinned against heaven and against you. I am no longer worthy to be called your son; make me like one of your hired servants.' So he got up and went to his father." ~ Luke 15:18-20a NIV

As we talked about previously, the prodigal son realized that he needed help and believed that his father could help him. So what does he do? He sets out for home. He plans to acknowledge his wrongs and throw himself at his father's mercy when he gets there. In the rest of the story, we see how that works out. It works out far better than he believes, but we'll get to that in the coming chapters. Right now, I want us to look at the choice being made and what the practical implications look like for him, as well as for the rest of us prodigal sons and daughters.

This third step of the journey we're on introduces a key difference from the ones that came before: action. It's about practical, in-the-moment forward movement. The previous steps have involved mental exercises—important ones, mind you—but the journey so far has been largely a matter of thought, hasn't it? We've reflected on, recognized, and *"come to our senses"* about our predicament. As a result of that recognition, we've understood that the solution must come from outside ourselves, right? We need to look to a higher power.

Well, this third step is about making the transition from analyzing the problem to taking a practical step toward the restoration we're desiring. So we read that he got up and went to his father. He's pretty committed to this course of action at this point, isn't he? Remember, he was starving to death, working feeding pigs in a far-off land. His decision to return to his father would've meant quitting his only source of income, grabbing whatever he had left, and hitting the road. There's not a lot of room to turn back. Is there? Probably a bit frightening for him. What was he really leaving, though? A series of bad decisions that left him destitute and no prospect of regaining any control. Doesn't sound like it's really that difficult a choice.

Why do you think he wouldn't have done it before then? Perhaps a little pride, not wanting to admit he was powerless and needed help. Can we relate to that? Ever find yourself looking at your decisions, going through steps one and two, but really struggling to give up that control and take the leap of faith that step three requires? I know I have. I don't like to give up that little bit of control I still believe I have and give it and my life to something else to trust. But what choice do we really have?

Why do you think the prodigal son and we have such a problem trusting that our higher power is up to the task and wants to help us? I would like to submit that we lack trust because we use ourselves as our model of God. By that, I mean that our picture of

God is controlled by our desires, our experiences, our thoughts, and our understandings rather than simply letting God be God. We put God in a box, limiting how we believe He can and should operate. Let's look at the story to understand this more.

"I will set out and go back to my father and say to him: Father, I have sinned against heaven and against you. I am no longer worthy to be called your son; make me like one of your hired servants.' So he got up and went to his father." ~ Luke 15:18-20a NIV

"I will say to him....I am not worthy.....make me a hired servant." That sounds reasonable, doesn't it? Sounds like he's owning his part, and his father would be fully justified to follow his suggestion. What else does it say about the father, though? How about that he would want to *lose a son to gain a servant*? That he wouldn't want his son to feel equal value in himself, at least to the fathers'? What about the idea that the father would even desire to think about consequences and not simply be delighted with the return of his lost son? *The son is painting his father into a box, isn't he?* He is imposing his own expectations on the situation as if their roles were somehow reversed.

How often do we do that? We complicate things. I always seem to believe that things are or should be more complicated than they really are or need to be. The prodigal son wasn't looking for the love of a father. A father who loved him so much that he would honor his son's inappropriate and downright disrespectful request for his inheritance before the father even died. He wasn't letting that love color his interpretation of his father's response when he returned home. It never even crossed his mind that his father would be happy to see and desire to restore him. The son believed things would be a lot more complicated. Ever done that?

I said earlier that this step calls us to give up control and trust in our higher power. We don't like to, but what choice do we have? It doesn't make a lot of sense to give up control in order to gain it. I would suggest that the confusion doesn't come from God, though, but from ourselves. We complicate it. We complicate it by believing that God is guided by our understanding, our way of doing things, and our perspective of justice rather than simply letting God be God. Isn't it a refreshing thought that there might be a different way to do things that we don't understand? Isn't there a bit of freedom in that?

To turn our will and our lives over to the care of God,...to give up control. That is, from a human point of view, a frightening prospect. I get it; I'm human. However, when we look back at our lives, it isn't such a new concept. We already did that, didn't we? We gave up control of our addictions, our compulsions, and our "sins."

So this step is simply calling us to give up control to someone who has our best interests at heart, unlike our previous masters. When we look at it in this light, doesn't it make sense to do it to align our will with God? Jesus, in speaking to those gathered around him, said:

"Come to me, all you who are weary and burdened, and I will give you rest. Take my yoke upon you and learn from me, for I am gentle and humble in heart, and you will find rest for your souls. For my yoke is easy and my burden is light." ~ Matthew 11:28-30 NIV.

You Take the Reins!

When two animals are yoked together to plow a field or pull a wagon, they work and accomplish their task together. If they were to pull in different directions, it would lead to disaster, wouldn't it? With that in mind, is it any surprise when we grab the wheel and try to steer in a different direction than God is leading that we end up in the ditch or over a cliff?

So, it sounds like taking this third step makes sense. Why do we balk, then? We stand at the edge of that precipice and insist on a safety line tying us to what we know. Why don't we rush to "turn our will and our lives over to the care of a loving God" and jump?

Well, it's kind of an "all-in" equation, isn't it? And that's the frightening part if we're truly honest with ourselves. We're being called to turn over all aspects of our lives, all our intentions, all our desires, all our hopes and dreams. We must trust that if they are changed or replaced, the new ones will be even better than what we came up with. That's the decision we're faced with. We may have to *change*.

Frightening but *freeing* as well. You see, we are not only deciding on our present and our future. We often don't stop to consider that our decision is also one about turning over our past. Remember, Jesus said, *"Come to me all who are weary and burdened, and I will give you rest."* You see, turning our will and lives over also means turning over the shame and guilt of the past, not to be buried under its weight anymore. That is what Jesus came for: to wipe the slate clean and allow us to live truly! That's why He went to the cross in our place. The prodigal son returned home expecting to face a father who would demand justice and consequences, *not one who was simply thrilled at his return and desired to forgive and restore him!*

That's the same kind of Father that this step asks us to turn our will and lives over to! We don't get to pick and choose what we turn over; it's all or nothing. We have to bet the farm. Our present, our future, and our past, He wants us to be free! When we look at what Jesus desires for us, how different that looks from the past we're leaving behind, is there any reason not to jump?

So, step three, as I indicated earlier, is where the rubber meets the road. From mental assent that we have a problem and that there can be a solution to deciding to seek that solution actively. We're faced with the choice to turn our wills and our lives over to God. Are you ready to do that today, tomorrow, and the next? This isn't a one-time thing. This is a choice that is made every day. As soon as the old eyeballs pop open in the morning, we need to turn it over and be willing to follow where we're led.

How do we do that? How do we learn to trust? Well, how do we get to know anyone? We talk to them, maybe read about them or read what they've written. Getting to know God is no different. All prayer is, is talking to God. We often shroud it in mystery and think it needs to have fancy language, but do you do that when you're trying to get to know a new friend? No, you simply talk to them and get to know them. When you think back on all the conversations you've had with friends, which ones stand out? The ones that helped shape and grow your friendship the most, I bet, were the ones where you trusted enough to be honest with them right? When you shared something that was going on with you or that you were struggling with, they were there for you. God is no different. He wants to hear what's on your heart and wants you to know that He's always right there beside you, always there when you need Him.

Therefore, the prodigal son in the story took the practical step and hit the road. He started the journey back to his father. As we consider what step three means to our journey together, we're faced with a decision as well. Am I going to continue to hold back and try to keep control of the wheel? Or am I going to turn my life and will over to Jesus? What action am I going to take today?

I encourage you to let go of the wheel and be amazed at how freeing that is, but the choice is up to each and every one of us. If you choose to let go of the wheel, whether for the first time or just simply for another day, it doesn't need to be anything complex. I said earlier that we always try to make things harder than they need to be. It's as simple as talking to God, acknowledging your need for Him, and asking for His help. If that is you, if you are ready to take that step, then I'd ask that you say a simple prayer with me, that you talk to God. There is no fanfare, no complex rituals, just you and God sharing some time together. You can pray aloud or quietly in your own heart; the choice is yours. Let's pray:

Heavenly Father, thank you for today. Thank you for loving me as a prodigal and refusing to turn Your back on me. Thank You for loving me so much, Jesus, that You would die for me on the cross. I am sorry for walking my own way, and I ask for Your forgiveness.

Please help me to walk with You today, tomorrow and evermore. In Your name, I pray, Jesus. Amen.

It's my sincere hope that you have decided to turn your life and your will over to God and take this next step of restoration. If you have made that choice, please let someone know. Strength is found in relationships. That's what God is all about: a robust relationship. Also, continue to pray daily and just talk to God. Whether it's when you get up, are driving your car, or sitting at work. Just talk to Him, get to know Him, and you'll be amazed at how He answers. Dig into the Bible as well. It's His Word that He's given us so we can know Him deeper. A word of caution: if you pray while driving, refrain from closing your eyes!

Exciting times! Like I said earlier, this is quite the journey we're on and we're only three steps down the road so far! :) Next, we start to really gain momentum as we engage in the restoration that He has planned for us.

Prayer

Heavenly Father, thank You for offering us freedom. Freedom from self, from our fears and our shame, freedom from our broken means of dealing with life. Please give us the courage to embrace Your promise to lead us into the much better life You desire and have planned for us. Amen.

Questions

1. How have I put God in a box, putting my expectations on Him? Am I willing to let Him out and be God?

2. Am I ready to turn my will and life over to the care of God instead of my addiction(s) and compulsion(s)? Am I ready to take my hands off the wheel?

Have I acted on my desire to change and accepted God's offer to help today? If not, why not do it now?

35

Chapter 4
Time to Take Stock

Ready to take the next step? This one can be a bit challenging but fear not. Jesus will walk you through it. Step 4 reads: *"We made a searching and fearless moral inventory of ourselves."*

On our journey thus far, we've been looking at a particular story in the Bible. The story of the Prodigal son that Jesus shares with His followers in Lk 15:11-31. When we look at it, there are many pieces to it that we can relate to, that line up with our own stories aren't there? Kinda amazing how something written two thousand years ago can still be relevant today. Let's read the story again so we can remember what has gone on and the steps we have taken so far.

"Jesus continued: "There was a man who had two sons. The younger one said to his father, 'Father, give me my share of the estate.' So, he divided his property between them. "Not long after that, the younger son got together all he had, set off for a distant

country and there squandered his wealth in wild living. After he had spent everything, there was a severe famine in that whole country, and he began to be in need. So he went and hired himself out to a citizen of that country, who sent him to his fields to feed pigs. He longed to fill his stomach with the pods that the pigs were eating, but no one gave him anything. "When he came to his senses, he said, 'How many of my father's hired servants have food to spare, and here I am starving to death! I will set out and go back to my father and say to him: Father, I have sinned against heaven and against you. I am no longer worthy to be called your son; make me like one of your hired servants."

So he got up and went to his father. "But while he was still a long way off, his father saw him and was filled with compassion for him; he ran to his son, threw his arms around him, and kissed him. "The son said to him, 'Father, I have sinned against heaven and against you. I am no longer worthy to be called your son.' "But the father said to his servants, 'Quick! Bring the best robe and put it on him. Put a ring on his finger and sandals on his feet. Bring the fattened calf and kill it. Let's have a feast and celebrate. For this son of mine was dead and is alive again; he was lost and is found.' So they began to celebrate."

Meanwhile, the older son was in the field. When he came to the house, he heard music and dancing, so he called one of the servants and asked him what was going on. 'Your brother has come,' he replied, 'and your father has killed the fattened calf because he has him back safe and sound.' "The older brother became angry and refused to go in. So his father went out and pleaded with him. But he answered his father, 'Look! All these years, I've been slaving for you and never disobeyed your orders. Yet you never gave me even a young goat so I could celebrate with my friends. But when this son of yours who has squandered your property with prostitutes comes home, you kill the fattened calf for him!' " 'My son,' the father said, 'you are always with me, and everything I have is yours. But we had to celebrate and be glad because this brother of yours was dead and is alive again; he was lost and is found.' " Luke 15:11-32 NIV

So far, we've looked at how the prodigal son and us, by extension, came to realize that in and of his own power, he wasn't able to control his life. He couldn't make the right choices, and how in fact, he always seemed to make the wrong ones. We've recognized also that *we* are powerless and that any solution must come from outside ourselves, from God. Last chapter, like the prodigal son who decided to turn to his father for help, we decided to turn to our Father *"God"* for help. To look to Him for guidance and strength to go through this life we've been given. We recognized that we would need help to continue walking on a new pathWe are now at the point of our journey where we're moving forward, where this journey of restoration gets some legs under it. In taking our fourth step, we're engaging the practical tools that will enable us to move to the succeeding steps. This and those to come will be a lot of work, but the rewards are amazing and life-changing if we take them. I'm excited to see what God does in our lives and where He takes us. So, are you ready to take the next step?

Step 4 is where *"We make a searching and fearless moral inventory of ourselves."* What is that exactly, how do we do it and why do we need to do it? An inventory is an accounting of something, isn't it? Businesses do an inventory to see what they have or don't have in stock. It's indispensable to keep a check. I remember back when I served as a kitchen manager a few years ago (that's me, jack of all trades, master of none!). One of the first things I did after starting was to do a thorough inventory to see what we had, how much we had, what we needed, and who our suppliers were. Doing that set the stage for any future development in the kitchen. Without doing so, it would've been tough to move forward. Well, this is really not much different. Step 4 is all about taking stock. Taking stock of ourselves, our past, and our present. What have we done? How has that affected others? What have our actions done to us? What is it about us today that seems to govern our actions and our responses? This is the time to pick a pen and paper and write down the stuff, which helps to identify things, their connections, and their effects more easily.

This whole process is meant to be a journey of restoration. Ever tried to put something from Ikea together without the instructions? We guys go, *"Bah, who needs instructions?"* but it's pretty difficult without them (and why is there always a piece or two left over?). We engage in this inventory so that we can identify actions that have led or continue to lead us on our old path. We do it so that we can identify what it is about our desires, our needs and wants that have led us on a voyage where we do not want to go anymore.

This can be a very painful process where we have to face things we'd rather not. In fact, not wanting to face them has probably been a large reason for some past behaviors, hasn't it? We've drank or used drugs or lashed out in anger or given control to someone else so that we could hide from the horrible things that would ask for self-realization. Then we did them again to hide from the shame of doing them in the first place. And the cycle continued, didn't it? Unless we identify something, it's pretty hard to change it. Ever want to repaint your car? Just going to the paint shop and talking to the salesman doesn't get it done. Unless you take him out to the parking lot and identify your car to him, it's pretty hard for anything to get done easily, isn't it? By identifying our hurts, actions and desires, by taking an inventory of them, we can begin to move forward toward the restoration we desire. We desire for our new path to be different, but unless we recognize what needs to change, how can we begin to change it?

In the story of the prodigal son, we were told that the son squandered his money on wild living and when a famine struck, he hired himself out to a local farmer feeding pigs. Remember we talked about how desperate he must have been. He was a Jewish man, subjecting himself to a non-Jewish boss and being around "unclean" animals. We talked about how this situation hadn't arisen overnight. It would've happened over time and he chose to ignore the bank statements coming in telling him that the money was running out. We're told in the story that a famine overtakes the land. Well, famines don't happen overnight. They are the result of a failed crop *season,* aren't they? So why didn't he act sooner and save himself? We've talked before about our amazing ability to self-deceive. The truth of the matter is that the son refused to look at what was going on. He refused to look at his actions and see where they were leading him. He refused to look in the mirror and admit what was happening under his watch.

We don't do that, ...do we? We don't refuse to look at ourselves and our actions and see where they take us, right? Often, we brush past the mirror, only take quick glances, and carry on. How often, when we're asked how things are going, do we throw up a mask and say "Great!" when really, on the inside, our lives are a mess? Perhaps we've even done these things today. Hmm, maybe that's how we got where we are.

In this story, we're told that the son "came to his senses" and recognized that he was "starving to death!" I picture him in the washroom one morning, at the sink, shaving. His focus is on the reflection in the mirror of the razor as it glides along, shaving cream disappearing, a trail of clean flesh appearing. Then, his view dials back a bit, and for the first time in a long time, he catches his entire reflection in the mirror. It suddenly strikes him with overwhelming thoughts of, "How on earth did I get here?" Perhaps it was the shadows in his sunken cheeks, the bags under his eyes, or the look of strain and sadness on his face. But for the first time, he actually holds his eyes on his reflection and takes stock of what he sees. It isn't pretty, *but* it does lead to the light coming on, doesn't it? As a result of his recognition, he is able to see the real story and start to take some action to address it.

Time to Take Stock

We're told he recognizes that he has sinned and is going to confess it to his father. The son in this story is in the process of taking the fourth step. We can call them moral failures, bad habits, or sins. The title doesn't matter. The son categorizes them as sin, so that is the term we'll use, but it doesn't really matter. What matters is that the son and us, take stock of our lives to this point, our actions, our desires, and our "sins." In doing that, we can identify things that would serve us better if they were changed.

If we're honest, there are two initial reactions we have to take an inventory such as this, and both are excuses not to do so. The first is pride— the belief that we don't need to change and that everyone else is the problem. Our actions are the result of what others have done to us—they need to change, not us! The second is fear that we're too afraid of what we'll discover, we're too afraid of change, and we're not up to the task. Both of these lines of reasoning I'm here to tell you, are bogus and will not serve us to continue on our journey of restoration. Both will sidetrack us, and like every lost person in the bush, we'll find ourselves wandering in circles, repeating the same old cycles. So commit to change, commit to walking forward and taking the next step in this journey.

If you don't think you're up to this step, you're right btw. That's why we're leaning on a higher power. It's in His strength that we're walking now. If the task seems to be off to a rough start, remember W, who is walking with you. Ask Him to open your eyes to what you need to identify and make a note of. Ask Him to help you face the fear of the unknown future, of where this journey is taking you.

Ask Him and He will answer because He is your loving Father God who wants you to move forward, to be restored to your original design and destiny. Now, I know that not everyone has had a good experience with their fathers. Some fathers have been downright terrible, abusive to, or abandoned us. So, the idea of trusting our heavenly Father is pretty hard to wrap our minds around and accept. I just encourage us to remember that our earthly fathers are just that—of the earth (world) and that the world is a fallen one. That's not an excuse, don't hear that. It's just a recognition of the situation we all find ourselves in. Our heavenly Father, however, is outside that. Remember, He loved us so much that He was willing to give up His Son for us. So please try to be open to the idea that this relationship could be different. If we're willing to trust, even just a little bit, I guarantee that He won't disappoint. Go ahead, give Him a chance. There's really not much to lose (we're already faced with the realization that we can't do this alone), and there is so much to gain!

The truth of the matter is that if we are not willing to do the work, the work will not get done (wow, that was a pearl of wisdom, wasn't it). It is true, though. Nobody else controls our lives. God promises to walk with us, guide us, and give us the strength to carry on when the going gets tough, but He won't do the work for us; that's our job. So whether it's fear of facing the decisions that have led us to where we are today or resentment towards others' actions that we blame for our problems, the choice falls wholly on us as to whether the journey continues or stalls here.

So what is it that we should be looking for, looking to identify? The list can be endless and use a whole bunch of terms. Probably the easiest way to categorize things, since the son says he's sinned, would be to refer to the list of the seven deadly sins, namely, pride, greed, lust, anger, gluttony, envy, and sloth. When we look at this story, which is only 20 lines long, we can find examples of each of these things surprisingly enough. Have I mentioned that we should all dig into the Bible because it has a wealth of wisdom to share?

The first thing to look for is *pride*. The son thought of himself as all that and a bag of chips at the beginning of the story. He thought he knew best how life should be lived. He thought his father owed him something. I mean, he went and demanded his father divide his possessions with him before he even died. Then once he got them, he ran off to live life his way, rather than staying under his father's care. How often do we think we're owed something? That we're a special case, the exception? How often do we think we know how best to do something, even if the prevailing wisdom says it should be done another way?

Greed — The son, as we just noted, looked at his father's possessions and wanted them for himself. He already had access to everything just by being the son. So why did he need to possess them? There's a difference between possessing something and simply borrowing it. Both allow us to have access, but possessing or owning something allows one to have control over it. That's what greed is about. The son wanted control of his destiny and the things in it. Well, by the end of the story, we see how much control he really had. How often do we desire to control things? How often do we look at stuff and want it, thinking that having it will give us more control over it and our lives?

Lust — The son, we're told, wasted his money on wild living, on prostitutes. He obviously struggled with the *"lust of the flesh"* and was willing to give up control of his finances and life to engage it. Besides lust of the flesh, however, lust can be tied to greed as we lust over "things." In Lynyrd Skynyrd's song "*Simple Man,*" a son is advised not to lust for rich man's gold. The prodigal son was guilty of lusting after his father's "gold" and was willing to break their relationship to gain it. How often do we put things ahead of the people around us, our families and friends? My workaholism led me down this particular path many times. How often do we look at someone else and undress them in our minds or engage in fantasy? How do we think we or those dearest to us would feel, if our thought lives were suddenly broadcast on a big screen for all to see? That's a terrifying thought, isn't it?

Anger — The older brother in this story was very angry that his father had welcomed his brother back. He was angry at what he believed was the unfair treatment of himself at the hands of his father. But where did that anger leave him? Outside the party. Outside his home. Remaining in a broken relationship with his lost brother. Don't get me wrong, the brother had every right to be angry, his brother had hurt the family. Perhaps his brother intended to apologize and beg his forgiveness along with his father though? The older brother won't know if he remains in his anger and lets it dictate his response. How often do we feel we've been wronged and decide to stay in our "righteous" anger and punish the other party by holding resentment against them? Actions have consequences, so I'm not saying everything should be forgiven and forgotten, but anger should not become a barrier to restoration. When it does, it is unrighteous then because for something to be righteous means it is in the right relationship with God, and God desires restoration, not the breaking of the relationship.

Gluttony - The son, we were told, engaged in wild living to the point of wasting all of his fortune. He spent everything. He didn't keep anything in reserve. You could say he lived in excess. We aren't like that, are we? How often do we want more? If we were to sit back and look at our situation and what we have, we'd realize that we already have enough. But we want more, don't we? Desiring things is not a bad thing. When we allow that desire to control us and negatively impact our well-being or those around us, however, then we're engaging in gluttony. If you have a roof over your head, some food in the fridge, and a bank account with only a couple of bucks in it, you're part of the top few percent of the wealthiest people in the world. Just something to think about when we're considering upgrading our 55" TV to a 70" because we feel we need a bigger picture.

Envy - The are a number of examples of envy in this story, and not all of them are bad. The son obviously was envious of his father's position and wealth at the beginning of the story. That's what led him to demand his "share" at the risk of breaking their relationship. The older brother is envious of the treatment given to his prodigal brother when he confronts his father about never receiving a party himself. Again, we can see how the brother's engagement in this feeling is actually stopping him from enjoying a party thrown by his father.

Now, we don't do these types of things, do we? We never look at our boss and demand a raise because the company had a successful year, even if it wasn't our department that was responsible. Or do we never look at a blessing given to a friend by someone and feel slighted because we didn't get something, too?

I said a moment ago that there is a good example of envy, and that might be stretching things a bit, but I think you'll understand what I mean. The son, while he's feeding the pigs, looks enviously at their food because he is hungry, we're told. Now, I say this is good envy because it prompts him to take some action (beneficial) to change his situation. Maybe it's not envy at all, but final recognition of his situation, but it leads him to take action. Do we do that sometimes, too? Look at something someone has, whether it's a possession or their health or whatever, and decide that we need to change something so we can enjoy those fruits as well.

The last of the seven deadly sins we need to look out for is *Sloth* - The prodigal son blew everything he had. We looked earlier at how this did not happen overnight. It wasn't a surprise. It wasn't a stock market crash but a sustained habit of ignoring the truth and failing to act. Call it laziness, procrastination, inability to face the truth, whatever. He didn't take any action to change the course he was on and ended up reaping the rewards, ...starving while feeding pigs. But we don't do that, do we? We won't open that bill that came in the mail? We don't put off having that discussion with our spouse or friend that would help us to be accountable? We don't go back for seconds and think to ourselves that we'll go to the gym tomorrow, right?

These are the things that this fourth step of our journey is calling us to look at in our lives. By taking the time to identify them, we can then have a starting point from which to move forward, engaging in change. When we look at the fifth step, we'll see how that change begins, and the process of restoration gains some breath of life. Right now, however, I want to leave you with two thoughts, one that speaks to our journey today and the other to tomorrow.

The first is this process of self-examination; this fourth step is like what I found myself doing in the kitchen one day at work. We had a box of green beans come in as a donation. They were from a local supplier and were nearing their expiration date, so that's why they were being donated. When we dug through them to prep them for supper, we found a few moldy ones in the mix, and we had to pick them out. We needed to go through the entire box, sorting and identifying the bad ones so they could be tossed and we could enjoy the good ones for supper. We were doing step 4 on this box of beans, identifying the bad stuff today so we could enjoy the rest.

The second thing I want to leave you with is that this process, step 4, not only serves us today but serves us tomorrow and for our the lifetime. As we identify things in our lives that lead us where we don't want to be, we get better at recognizing them in the future. We come to identify them early enough to take action and avoid them before they sidetrack us again. So, I encourage you to dig into this fourth step, and spend some time thinking about past behaviors, what motivates you, and the consequences of your actions. Consider these things, and spend some time in prayer asking for guidance in identifying them. Ask God to give you some insight, and some clarity, so that you can begin to pick the bad beans out and enjoy the fruits of your labours! God bless you on your journey!

Prayer

Heavenly Father, please give us the courage and insight to look at ourselves, our past, our motivations, our actions, and our patterns so that we can put pen to paper and start to put legs under our recovery. Amen.

Questions

1. Am I ready to do the hard work of looking at my life, identifying the issues I've had and actions I've taken that have brought me to where I am today?

2. Pen and paper time. What actions have I engaged in in the past? Pride, Greed, Lust, Anger, Gluttony, Envy, Sloth? Take time to identify and write them down.

3. How have these shaped what came next? How did they affect me? Others? Are there common themes that seem to run through my past and present?

Chapter 5
I Did It

So, step 5, this is a big one. We're really putting rubber on the road at this point in our journey. This next step is:

"We admitted to God, to ourselves and to another human being the exact nature of our wrongs."

A bit frightening, isn't it? Admitting or confessing something really puts them in your face. Okay, we can decide to confess something to God. He's all about forgiveness, so that has the prospect of going well. Admitting something to ourselves may be hard, but we can struggle through that. But admitting our deepest, darkest secrets to someone else—a living, breathing person who can think and judge like we do? That's pretty terrifying. If we're really honest, we'd probably prefer to do anything else but that!

When we get to this step, I think it's good to remember why we started this journey. What are we hoping and striving for? The subtitle of this book is "Life Steps — A Prodigal Journey." It's not

"Life Steps —A journey from A to B" or "Life Steps —A Tourist's Guide to Heaven." If you remember, we set out on this journey with the recognition that life had become unmanageable and that we were powerless to change that ourselves. It was that humbling recognition that, left to our own devices, we screw things up that led us to start this journey. We wanted something more, and these steps, this twelve-step journey, when taken seriously and acted upon, tantalized us with a promise of restoration, didn't it? So, when faced with the frightening prospect of confession today, in this fifth step, I encourage you to take heart and trust in the journey. Trust in the promise of *restoration* and the promise of Jesus to be *with us* each step of the way. It's alright to be scared; that is a natural instinct meant to awaken us and prepare us to respond and act upon things. Being scared is only bad when it immobilizes us and doesn't allow us to take appropriate action. So, in entering into this, we need to embrace our fear, carry it with us, and allow it to propel us to take the next step forward. If we're not a bit afraid, I'd have to question how honest we're being. Are we really putting anything on the line, risking anything on the promise of something better?

So, with that being said, let's get going. We started this journey with the recognition that we needed help and that this help must come from outside ourselves. Whenever we ran things, we found ourselves on a road to nowhere. We came to believe that perhaps God had a better roadmap than us *if* we would allow ourselves to take some direction. Now as a guy (and my lovely wife can attest to this), I know that is a tough thing to do, to pull over and ask for directions. We never get there unless we do, though, right?

So we decided to give our lives into the care of God, to follow His roadmap. The decision was made— not our will, but Your will be done—and we're going to trust in the process (that's faith, by the way).

So, what was our first question once we got on board? What was the step that led us here today? "*We made a searching and fearless moral inventory of ourselves.*" We looked at our pasts and tried to objectively identify places we'd gone off the path, hurting ourselves and others. Places where we consciously and unconsciously choose to exercise our will, not the will of a loving God. We looked at what is about us that seems to guide our actions and lead us astray. Getting honest with ourselves and really looking in the mirror was a scary step, too, wasn't it? Perhaps we hadn't looked at our reflection for quite some time and were afraid of what we might find. But we had resolved to trust in the process, to trust in the One who can see better than us. It wasn't ultimately as bad as you thought, was it? Our fear didn't paralyze us; God didn't abandon us. We're still on this path of restoration and looking forward to the brighter future promised to us.

I once put a quote up on Facebook from the conference I attended. I think it speaks to the trust we need if we're going to continue this journey we're on. It's from a guy named Louie Giglio, whom you may have heard of before. He said, "*You don't need to know everything about climbing the mountain in front of you to take the next step.*"[3]. We don't need to understand how this is working, or how the coming steps in this journey will accomplish our goal. In fact, if we could truly map out this journey ourselves, why would we need God? And so, while you mull that thought over, here's another: how did the last time you didn't need God work out? Just a question. So I encourage you as we take this next step today, to trust in the process, to have faith. This is a journey of *restoration.* Embrace it with the fervor of a starving man at a banquet table!

"*We admitted to God, to ourselves, and to another human being the exact nature of our wrongs.*" Why do we take this step? And I mean, for what reasons besides that we trust in the process as we just discussed. Well, this series has been all about looking at the twelve steps and their Biblical foundations, so that seems an appropriate place to look for an answer. So, what does the Bible have to say about this topic? It's pretty clear-cut, actually. Whether you look at the story of John the Baptist, the actions of believers in the Book of Acts, or in the letter from James to believers, everywhere in the New Testament, you'll find accounts of believers confessing their sins to each other and to God. In James, we're even explicitly commanded to do so:

"Confess your sins to each other and pray for each other so that you may be healed." ~ James 5:16 NLT

We can see from scripture that this is an encouraged and expected practice.

Besides being a directive from God, however, why else would we want to confess? What is it hoping to accomplish? If we look at the command we're given in James, we get a glimpse of why we're to do this. James 5:16 reads: "*Confess...so that you may be healed.*" So that we may be healed! Remember, we're on a journey of restoration. We're looking to be restored to something, to be healed and regain a former glory. If we break an arm or a leg, we cast it and eventually go to some physio. We go to him because the doctor says we should go, and we trust his judgment. But ultimately, we go because we want to be healed, to regain our strength and use of our limb right? We want to be restored to our former abilities. This step five, confessing, is no different. We want to heal from our past actions and negate future missteps.

So how does that happen? What does the physiotherapist get us to do? Specific exercises meant to restore each of the muscles in our arm or leg. This step similarly guides us to exercise each of the pieces involved in our transgressions (that's a fancy word for screw-ups btw). In doing so, they can be restored and become healthy again. We're told to confess to God, ourselves, and to another human being. Those three relationships are the "muscles" we need to move and bring back to life, and confession is the exercise that does so.

Confess to God. I think this is probably the easiest muscle to exercise in this step in some ways. Perhaps because God can seem a bit more nebulous, He is not a finite being standing in front of us, looking into our eyes. We also have to consider that since God is all-knowing, he already knows our sins. So it's not like it's a big revelation to Him. Is it when we confess them?

Why is it as hard as it is sometimes to do this step, then? Perhaps we find it hard to believe that we can be forgiven. That even God, with all His grace and mercy, would have a hard time looking past what we've done. I get that. Been there. Perhaps, however, if we look at that just a bit closer, we will see another truth emerge. *I'm so bad. I've done stuff so terrible that even God cannot possibly hear my confession and desire to continue with me!* Even God... Who are we to put a limit on God? Are we God? Does this not smell a little suspicious? Maybe there's still a little whiff of pride in the air. Perhaps then, the act of confession highlights to us that we are not God, which can help us understand Him a bit more. We ask ourselves, how can He forgive? In light of our knowledge of Him and how He is different than us and loves us eternally, the question I submit should be, how can He not forgive? You can be encouraged by that realization!

The act of confession, in my understanding, is two parts. The first is an unburdening of ourselves of weight and perceptions or masks that dictate our road forward. The second is the power of witness which I'll talk about in a bit. When we confess something, it's like we take a piece of heavy clothing off and set it down. It sits there, exposed for all to see and inspect. It now becomes its own entity. Before, it was Brad's jacket. I was wearing it, living in it. Now, there is a jacket on the floor. It still belongs to or can be associated with me, but I am not carrying the weight of it anymore. I am not being directly influenced or constrained by it am I? As we confess our wrongs to God, ourselves, and another person, like clothing, we shed each piece. We take off the burden of the lies and secrets that, until that point, restricted us and controlled our path forward. How did these things control us before, and dictate what we could do? Well, ever lie about a need to someone? Ever say a bill needs to get paid and then blow the gift on something else? We probably avoided the person we borrowed from for a while right? So we wouldn't have to lie and perhaps, heaven forbid, get caught in that lie about what we did with the money? When we finally confess something, the truth is out there; it might hurt and cause us some shame, but our paths forward suddenly increase exponentially. That path to a restored relationship suddenly becomes available again. It may be a bit rough, but access has been granted again!

Confess to ourselves. This one can be pretty hard. Why do you think sometimes it's easier to forgive others than it is to forgive yourself? Well, we're pretty close to the carnage we've caused. All we need to do is turn around and look at our path behind us and see all the mistakes we've made, all the relationships we've hurt, all the lies we've told.

When we look at someone else and what they've done to us, we can somehow differentiate between them and their actions, can't we? We can still see their value and recognize that their actions didn't match their value, so they can be separated and set aside or forgiven.

As I said, we're perhaps too close to our carnage, making it pretty difficult. So what do we often do? A couple of things. One, we try to rationalize away some of the things we've done. They weren't that bad or they were the result of what someone else did to me. Whatever the rationalization, deep down, we know the truth, and in doing this, we just add one more secret to the pile, don't we? Secondly, we try to make up for things. We strive harder to be better, to make amends, to balance the scale. We look back and count the bad things and then move forward, trying to do good things so it'll all even out in the end. How well do we think that works? All we need to do is turn around and look again to see the new stuff on the path we have to make up for, and we realize that we can never catch up.

Obviously, neither of these solutions is going to solve our dilemma. So we're back to confessing to ourselves. Instead of trying to justify, hide, or repay our screw-ups, why don't we just face them? Call them out of the dark and into the light of day. We acknowledge our part in them by admitting them and wiping the slate clean to start afresh. You don't have to let the weight of lies and excuses dictate the paths forward anymore!

Confess to another human being. I am sure that everyone who has ever undertaken this journey has asked the question why? Why do I need to air all my dirty laundry with another person? Our logic runs something like this:

1. If God is the master of the universe,

2. and ultimately, all things I've done are sin against him

3. and I can admit this stuff to Him and myself (the other person who was there when all of this stuff went down),

4. Then why do I need to drag in a third party and relive the shame with them?

Why indeed? Here, in this final confession, I believe lies one of the greatest benefits of this step. In fact, without this being addressed, I don't know how successful the rest of the journey could be. It's that serious.

What is, ultimately, one of the major factors that lead us to deal with life in unhealthy ways? Now, these unhealthy things may involve the use of drugs or alcohol, lying, or overeating, or becoming codependent, and the list goes on and on. We just need to look behind us to see what these things look like in our own lives. So again, I ask the question, what is one of the main factors that lead us to unhealthy lives? Loneliness. Isolation. A feeling of not belonging, of being apart. This part of step five addresses the lie of the enemy. Confessing to God and ourselves do this as well. However, confessing to another person supplies us with the tangible proof that we no longer need to believe the lie that we are not a part of something. By admitting our wrongs to another person and their not running away screaming and damning us, we are restored to a relationship with *humanity* through the flesh and blood representative sitting before us. We are no longer the monster looking in through the window at the rest of the people. We are accepted as we are and are welcomed back into life with others. That is so powerful! A word of advice on your choice of who to confess to. As I've indicated, this step is truly freeing and necessary. That said, it is not one to rush into and confess to anyone. Some of our past hurts may be from trusting someone, and they let us down by sharing something that was said in confidence. We need to exercise wisdom in choosing who it is that we confess to. I'd suggest it be a counselor, pastor, or sponsor if you've joined an A group. I suggest these because these individuals are all professionals or have firsthand experience (as in the case of a sponsor), know the sensitive nature of this endeavor, and will keep your confidence. If you have not plugged into a community (faith-based or step group), this may be the perfect time to do so. By joining a group of like minded individuals, you can find support and fellow travelers to share your journey with you. Remember, our struggles tend to lead us into isolation. Joining a community helps us proactively address this issue before it even becomes one.

Now, a little bit ago, I said there were two important things about confession, two pieces to it, if you will. The first was the unburdening of ourselves and the freedom to choose a different path from that point on. The second, the power of witness, I said I would get back to. To witness something is to see it and to be able to attest to it as having happened. Like being a witness to a crime or the witnessing of a signature. When we dig into this step and admit to God, to ourselves, and to another human being the exact nature of our wrongs, what are we left with? If we picture the act of confession, like the stripping off of clothes one at a time until everything has been unloaded, what are we left with? Our naked bodies - just us, nothing else. No lies, no baggage, no secrets, no masks; just us and three witnesses. God, ourselves, and other human being get to see us as we truly are and the value we inherently hold as children of God. As if that's not enough, the even bigger miracle happens — we get to witness our *acceptance* and *restoration* into our relationship with God, ourselves, and humanity. That's the power of this step; that's the restoration we're all seeking. That's the miracle that happens when we trust and take the next step forward. We get to truly see and witness our value and never have to question it again. So, are you in?!?

We've been looking at a particular story in the Bible so far, the story of the Prodigal son. Do you remember where to find it? Lk 15:11-31. I told you by the end of this journey, you're going to shout out Luke 15:11-31 whenever you hear a reference to the story of the Prodigal son.

We've looked at how the son realized he needed his father's help, recognized how he'd wronged him, and done an inventory of his life. He had decided to return to his father, confess his sins, and throw himself at his father's mercy. That's where I'd like to pick up the story from. Beginning in Lk 15:20:

"So he got up and went to his father. "But while he was still a long way off, his father saw him and was filled with compassion for him; he ran to his son, threw his arms around him and kissed him. "The son said to him, 'Father, I have sinned against heaven and against you. I am no longer worthy to be called your son.' "But the father said to his servants, 'Quick! Bring the best robe and put it on him. Put a ring on his finger and sandals on his feet. Bring the fattened calf and kill it. Let's have a feast and celebrate. For this son of mine was dead and is alive again; he was lost and is found.' So they began to celebrate." ~Luke 15:20, 21, 23, 24 NIV

So the son takes step five, doesn't he? He goes to his father and admits his guilt. He admits that he's wronged God, his dad, and himself. He admits to himself that he's the one at fault, that he blew the life he could've had because now he's looking at a life of servitude. He comes before his father and unloads himself. He strips off his clothes, so to speak, the lies, the hurts, the secrets, baring himself before God, himself, and another person, and what happens? Do you think it's any coincidence that his father first tells the servants to bring his son the finest robe, a ring, and sandals? In that culture, those are symbols of who he is, the family he belongs to, and his status as a son. His father instructs the servants to kill the calf they'd been preparing for a worthy celebration. Do you think it's any coincidence that such a celebration is meant to include everyone? The father says that his son was lost but has now been found! Can there be any more of a picture of the restoration to be found in how admitting our wrongs opens up paths that were closed before?

There is one last thing I'd like us to look at from this story today. The son, when he came to realize his situation and decided to head home, what was his belief? You'll find it in his confession. He believed that he no longer had a place at his father's table, that he was no longer a son, and didn't belong anymore. And what is it we first find his father doing?

"But while he was still a long way off, his father saw him…" Lk 15:20

He was out there scanning the horizon, looking for his son. His *son*. No question he believed his son still belonged to the family, is there? What the son believed was the lie of the enemy. When you think you've blown it, he pounces on that and feeds you that lie that you don't belong. That what you've done is unforgivable and that you've been cast out. You need to remember who has *been cast out and that you have a father* searching for you. He is waiting for you to appear on the horizon so he can assure you of His love and that you belong to Him; nothing changes that. So take heart, my fellow traveler, as we continue to walk down this path. We belong here; our Father has laid the stones ahead of us and is walking side by side with us. What more can we ask for?

Prayer

Heavenly Father, please give us the courage to confess to you, to ourselves, and to another flesh and blood human being. Help us to take this step and experience the freedom and restoration You desire for us to walk in. Amen.

Questions

1. Am I ready to take this step and share at a level I may never have before? Do I believe doing so will change my life's journey?

2. Who is it that I will confess to? Identify and ask this person to help you with this step of your journey.

3. How has the enemy lied to me about my sense of belonging, about being a child of God? How will I respond now when he tries to lie to me again?

Chapter 6
Get Ready, Get Set...

In this chapter we will be looking at the sixth step in our journey. Step 6 is both exciting and terrifying at the same time. It is fairly straightforward and simple, yet sometimes the simplest things are the hardest, aren't they? Step 6 reads:

"Were entirely ready to have God remove all these defects of character."

Before we explore this new step, we should quickly retrace the steps that have led us here. That will help us to truly embrace the challenge laid out before us in this step. So far, we've recognized that in our own strength, we're sunk. We end up doing what we don't want and don't do what we want to do, right? We discovered that if there is going to be a solution to our seeming to always end up on the wrong path, it must come from outside ourselves. We chose to turn to God for our marching orders from now on.

We've looked deep inside ourselves, tried to understand what drives us, how we've blown things and hurt those around us and ourselves. The last step we took was to confess all that stuff to ourselves, to God, and to another person – and we found it was freeing! We're no longer outsiders looking in, but we're now part of something bigger. We belong now, don't we?

Forgive me if I seem to be rushing through these past 5 steps. Having taken five chapters to dig into them, a few sentences don't really do them justice. I just want to trace a broad picture of our journey so far. We have come a long way from the desperation leading us to step 1. It has all just been the prelude, the prologue to where we find ourselves now – step 6:

"Were entirely ready to have God remove all these defects of character."

In the last step, we aired all our dirty laundry; we've recognized it, detailed it, shared it, and are looking to move beyond it. This next step is about being ready for God to help us. You're ready, right? Let's get to it! God, please remove these defects of mine that always seem to drag me off Your path. Help me to stay on the road and stop taking these detours through the ditch.

Ever tried to make a deal with God? You know, sometimes when we find ourselves up against the wall, and we send out one of those desperate prayers – "Lord, if You get me out of this, I promise I'll…" (you fill in the blank from what you remember). Then we promptly did it again. We weren't really ready to change, were we?

Before we look into that part of our nature further, let's look at what exactly this step says first. The problem identified in this step is that we have defects in our character. So what are they? We explored them somewhat in the last 2 steps but there is a lot more to them than what we've already identified.

Defects of character. What is character anyway? Our character is made up from, or based upon our desires and the actions we take to achieve those desires. When we say that someone is of good character, we say that their actions have historically lined up with their words and heart. Based on both, their desires seem to be focused on being beneficial rather than a detriment to those around them. If we say that someone is a scoundrel and of bad character, that is usually based on our observation of their behaviour. We've observed that they are self-centered and do not act in the best interest of the community at large.

Therefore, we need to look at what has been our character in the past. Have we ever driven off into the ditch of self-centeredness? Based on what we identified of our pasts in step 4, have we been of good character or have we been scoundrels? I'm not trying to beat you up here or point any fingers; I'm just as guilty as the next person. My past has been "colourful" with lots of off-roading. And if I'm totally honest, my "colourful past" is probably as fresh as last week! So, we all have defects of character. But how do we determine them, how do we pin them down so we can understand them and hopefully drag them kicking and screaming into the light? Once we've identified them, how do we measure them? This will become very important if we want to stay on this journey of restoration in the future. In fact, it's so important that unless we are able to do this, our journey will end here. I'll address this more comprehensively a little later.

It has been said that character defects can be understood as the distance between where God would see our character and where we actually are. Let me repeat that – character defects can be understood as the distance between where God would see our character and where we actually are. So where would God like to see our character? Our character is meant to line up with His. For clarity on what His character is like, we just need to look to the example of His Son, Jesus, to see what our sights should be set on. Read the Gospels and see how He lived. Matthew, Mark, Luke, and John are records of His life and how He lived and breathed. How He loved and cried. How He lived and how He died. His life was meant as a model for us – love each other, serve each other, put others before ourselves. Stand up to injustice, seek truth. Value relationships and community. This is why you'll hear me time and again encouraging you to dig into your Bible because it's our instruction manual for life!

Earlier in the journey, we looked at what has been identified as the seven deadly sins, including pride, greed, lust, anger, gluttony, envy, and sloth. Use these as a guide when looking at our lives. Are any of these driving your actions and forming your character into something other than what God desires for you?

So, like I said earlier, we're ready to take this next step. God, please come and take away these defects of character. They have ruled us too long and kept us from our desired lives. We're ready for change! …Or are we?

We've been looking at the story of the prodigal son and seeing how he came to terms with his past and walked this same journey of restoration that we've embarked on. I want us to look again at that story and see what it can tell us about this step 6 we're exploring now. You'll remember that the prodigal son had demanded that his father give him his inheritance early. He then ran off and squandered it on wild living in a far-off country. He became so destitute that he was starving to death, working to feed pigs while looking hungrily at their slop. He finally came to his senses, didn't he? He decided to return home and become a servant for his father. Upon returning, his father surprised him by restoring him as a son, not taking him in as a servant. They held a great party to celebrate the return of this lost son. This is where I want to pick up the story. Do you remember where to find this story and what the reference to it is? Lk 15:11-32. So, picking up at the party, Luke chapter 15, verse 25:

25 "Meanwhile, the older son was in the field. When he came near the house, he heard music and dancing. 26 So he called one of the servants and asked him what was going on. 27 'Your brother has come,' he replied, 'and your father has killed the fattened calf because he has him back safe and sound.'

28 "The older brother became angry and refused to go in. So his father went out and pleaded with him. 29 But he answered his father, 'Look! All these years I've been slaving for you and never disobeyed your orders. Yet you never gave me even a young goat so I could celebrate with my friends. [30] *But when this son of yours who has squandered your property with prostitutes comes home, you kill the fattened calf for him!'*

[31] *"'My son,' the father said, 'you are always with me, and everything I have is yours.* [32] *But we had to celebrate and be glad, because this brother of yours was dead and is alive again; he was lost and is found.'"*

We have to sympathize with the older brother a bit. I mean, he's been faithful to his father, slaving away, doing what needed to be done, following his father's direction. Meanwhile, his brother has been out living it up! And what has all his hard work gotten him? Well, according to him, nothing. His father has never so much as given him a young goat to have with his friends. So he gets angry and refuses to go to the party. And what does it get him? At the very least, he misses out on yet another party, doesn't he?

There's a line in the center of all this stuff going on for the brother that is very important. We breeze over it perhaps a bit too quickly and easily because it seems to be there to set up the next piece of the brother's response. Let's look at the second half of verse 28 again. *"So his father went out and pleaded with him."* He pleaded with him. His father is trying to accomplish something here that we need to pay attention to. Is he trying to smooth things over so the party can go on? Is he demanding that his oldest son suck it up and get in there with the rest of the family? No, he is continuing to do exactly what he's been doing all his son's life – to teach him about life. He's striving to shape him into a person of good character, not a scoundrel. He reaffirms his love for his son, and reaffirms that all he has belongs to the son. He acknowledges that his son has worked hard and it is due him. But, he also encourages, nay pleads with his son to recognize that some things are so much beyond that. The restoration of a brother that was lost is one of those things. The older brother we read refuses to learn this newfound lesson and continues to drive off into the ditch of self-centeredness. I believe this is a picture of the difficulty facing us as we strive to take this sixth step on our journey. The father is striving to encourage his son, and by extension, us, to move from an attitude of entitlement to one of gratitude. To look beyond himself/ourselves and to look to the benefit of others.

We want to change, don't we? We've come so far. We want a new life. We're ready for God's help to change things and chart a new course. But what did the older brother do in this story? He refused to learn the lesson his father was trying to teach him. Oh, he was ready to work on life; he wasn't like his younger brother, who wanted it all at once. No, the older brother had worked faithfully for years, learning from his father and building on his newfound skills. He's been working the farm, building his character through his words and actions. But in this critical moment, he grabbed the wheel again, didn't he? We don't do that... do we?

We're at a point now where we're looking forward to the rest of this journey, but if we're honest, we have it plotted out a bit already, right? We kinda have a plan of how this is going to work, what we need to work on, and what needs to change. We've caught a glimpse of what life could look like when God takes away the junk that keeps messing things up. If that's us, then I'm sorry to say that we're not ready. We're the older brothers in the story, picking and choosing what we will or will not learn. It's only a matter of time before we find ourselves off-roading again, wondering how we can get back out of the ditch. Sorry if that sounds harsh, but the truth hurts sometimes.

This step says: *"We are entirely ready to have God remove all these character defects."* Entirely ready – that means there's no picking and choosing. No putting off. No deciding that something is off limits. Here's a litmus test to see if you're truly ready. When faced with something in yourself, character defects that you desire to change, what is your motivation? Is the desire to change driven because the price of the consequences is getting too high? Or is it because you want to be a better person? Remember, character defects are the distance between where God would see our character and where we actually are. Where God would see – that's the most essential part of the equation. We cannot see, not truly. True character change is not about avoiding consequences; it's about becoming good as we're led and transformed by a good Father.

We've identified some things in the last couple of steps, but those things are just like the lessons the older brother chose to learn because he could see that they would benefit him. The lessons we need to learn that we cannot see are the most important. Those things form the foundation of our character and serve to set us up for the rest of our lives. We've proven that we cannot see them, so we've turned to God for help. Now, it's up to us to be willing to take on the task, whatever that may be that He calls us to. Nothing is off-limits. No picking and choosing. We need to be entirely ready to respond to God's direction, whatever it may be. So I put the question to you – are you ready? If so, get ready for a roller coaster ride because we all have much shaping for God to do. However, we can be secure in the knowledge that whatever He asks of us, He walks beside us through it.

When you ponder this question of readiness and find yourself questioning, don't lose heart. The prodigal son's father didn't abandon the older brother because he refused to join in right then. His father assured him that everything was still his. We're not told the rest of the son's story, but we know the author and His story as told in the Gospels. That leads me to believe that He was ultimately successful at helping His son*s* take the next step.

Take some time, read the Gospels, and get to know Your heavenly Father. See how He lived and write some of those lessons in your heart so you can live as He calls us to.

Prayer

Heavenly Father, please give us the courage to trust in You and that you desire the best for us. Help us to take this step up faith and walk forward with You. Amen.

Questions

1. Am I *entirely* ready to have God remove my character defects?

2. Do I trust God to lead me, and am I willing to walk even when I can't see where or why?

3. How well do I know the Father and Jesus, His character that I want to line up with? Commit to read the gospel accounts of His life and get to know Him better.

Chapter 7
Bang! And We're Off!

Yahoo, we're over the hump and on the downhill stretch! Take a minute to congratulate yourself on sticking with this. It's been a tough slog so far, but as we crest this hill, the goal does seem a little closer, doesn't it? So take heart, resist the urge to coast, and continue with Step 7.

"Humbly asked Him to remove our shortcomings."

That doesn't sound that bad, does it? This is what we've been working towards. So far on our journey, we've recognized that we cannot do this alone and need God's help. Instead of looking the other way or only taking fleeting glimpses, we've grabbed the mirror and taken a good look at ourselves. We didn't really like everything we saw. But we stared at our reflection, refusing to run away as we used to, didn't we? We even took a step to admit what we've done, what drives us to do things. We admitted these things to not only God and ourselves but to another person. We've experienced the restoration, the sense of no longer being an outsider looking in, that came with that confession. Lastly, we really dug in to discover if we were truly ready to have God remove these shortcomings from us. We talked about what that looked like. If you remember, it's one thing to want to change because you're tired of living with the consequences of your actions. It's entirely another however, to want to change because you want to become a better person. We also explored the repercussions of what that type of change may require. Openness. Trust. Patience. Open to allowing God to be the architect, not ourselves. Trusting that He is capable and faithful to complete the work in our lives. Patient in our efforts to simply take it one step at a time as He puts things in front of us. We talked about our being truly ready to do whatever it takes to change whatever God identifies in us. That is the natural springboard into today's step (imagine that, a step following the one before it; you'd think they were planned that way).

"Humbly asked Him to remove our shortcomings." You know, I liken our journey so far to that of an army getting ready for battle. An army needs to look at itself, and make critical assessments as to what it needs, where its weakest points are, and what supplies etc it needs. An army looks to its generals for its marching orders. The people in the trenches cannot see the overall battle plan nor how the battle develops. They need to trust those in command to guide them, to move the pieces into position to achieve the ultimate goal. Those soldiers in the trenches have a choice to make. Will they trust in their leaders and be ready to do what they're directed to do? Or are they going to follow their own ideas? An effective army marches to the beat of a single drum. Poised on the brink of battle, the army

with the best chance for victory is the one whose soldiers are ready and committed to doing what needs to be done. Its soldiers trust in the larger plan of their commanders and are ready to enter the battle. That's the point we were at last step. That's the question each of us has to wrestle with: are we ready to do what our commander, Jesus, asks of us? If it doesn't look like we thought it would or gets really uncomfortable, are we truly willing and ready to trust that He knows best for us and follow?

Today is March Out Day—time to saddle up and ride. Today is where this journey goes from one of mental prep and agreement to putting one boot in front of the other and walking forward as He directs. *"Humbly asked Him to remove our shortcomings."* That seems very straightforward, doesn't it? Ask Him to take all this junk from us that we've identified. *"Please, God, take it away; I'm tired of dealing with all this stuff. I can't do it in my own strength, I need Your help."* The first part of this step reads *"Humbly asked...".* What does that mean? Do we need to grovel and beat ourselves up? We've already identified that we can't do life in our own strength. Is God demanding that we acknowledge His supremacy again, just in case we forgot or took back a bit of our will again? I suppose recognizing our weaknesses is always a part of it, but certainly not the main focus He highlights in this step. Asking humbly is all about shaping or forming our hearts. We need to remember that God is the potter and that we are the clay.

This whole journey we're on is one of restoration. Restoration to what, though? Restoration to the design that God has had for us all along. He sees in us the person He designed before the universe was even created. He is the one who can mold us, form us, and transform us into that image. Michelangelo once said, "Each piece of marble was a finished work of art, just waiting for the sculptor to chip away the extra stone and reveal it to the world." That is how God sees us. By humbly asking, we start the journey of becoming transformed more and more into His image. Humility is core to the character of God.

In his letter to the believers in Philippi, Paul highlights the humility Jesus demonstrated.

"Who, being in very nature God, did not consider equality with God something to be used to his own advantage; rather, he made himself nothing by taking the very nature of a servant, being made in human likeness. And being found in appearance as a man, he humbled himself by becoming obedient to death— even death on a cross!" ~ Philippians 2:6-8 NIV

So what is it about humility that God so wants us to learn? Why is it such an integral part of His character? We need to remember that our God has a servant's heart. A servant is someone who puts those being served ahead of themselves. Does that mean we are to question our value, to recognize that others are worth more, and fall in line where we should be? Some of us may even struggle with our sense of value with self-hatred. Is this step indicating that we're right to believe these things? I pointed out just a minute ago that *no*, that is not the case. We are all works of art in God's eyes. We need to remember that He sees value in us. He sees value in *you*.

There must be something more going on here, then. Perhaps some history will shed some light on what God is trying to help us identify in this step. Do you know another name? The angel Lucifer/Satan was called another name before he was cast out of heaven: "The Angel of Light" — he was the most beautiful angel. What was he cast out for? Trying to take over heaven, to replace God. We need to consider what was it that led him to try and take over? Pride. He came to believe that he didn't need God. He believed that he could take care of things on his own. Yes, Satan's great undoing was pride. Now, we don't struggle with pride,... do we? In our past, we didn't think we could control things. What was step one all about again?

That being said, then, we dealt with pride back in step one. What does it have to do with this step? Well, we need to remember that this is all about a *journey* of restoration. The twelve steps of AA, NA, etc, are focused initially on dealing with an addiction. Whether it's alcohol or drugs or something else, there's an "_A" group for it out there. That is just the simplest piece of the puzzle this journey is trying to help us address. If we hope to remain "sober" or on the right path and achieve any lasting happiness in life, we need to address our whole lives. We need to look at all of our character defects, which means addressing the issue of pride wherever it pops its ugly head up.

Did you know that one of the chief architects of pride is a desire to be self-reliant? We're not meant to be self-reliant. We're communal beings by nature; we're not meant to be alone. Don't believe me? Look at the One who made us in His image—three in one: Father, Son, and Holy Spirit. God Himself is a communal being. We can understand how sometimes self reliance has been born out of our experience in life. Perhaps we've been constantly let down by people, by our families even, maybe from as far back as childhood. We can decide that we'll never rely on someone else again, so we won't experience that pain again. But do we realize that in doing so, we're falling for the same trap that ultimately led the Angel of Light to be cast out of heaven?

So being humble, being a servant, is not about recognizing where we belong in the order of things like a class system. It's all about putting guardrails in place to ensure we stay on track and not fall into the trap of pride. It's about approaching our lives with an attitude that combats pride before it can even start. If we're always looking to serve those around us, it's a bit hard to develop a sense of entitlement. Think about it: what are we entitled to if everyone is before us? This step is not about subjugating ourselves and never looking after ourselves, so don't hear me say that. This is all about determining our approach to life and to the change that God calls us to as we ask Him for his help. As I said earlier, this is all about shaping our hearts so that they lead us to be transformed more and more into what God designed us to be.

There is a passage in Isaiah that is both an instruction and a promise. I believe it can help us understand our road and the bright future God has planned for us. It's found in Isaiah chapter 57, verse

14:

"God says, Rebuild the road! Clear away the rocks and stones so my people can return from captivity."

God is telling His people, *us*, to risk the journey, to tackle the task at hand, and take the next step. We're to rebuild the road, our life that has fallen into disrepair. We're to take each step as it comes, facing the big problems, the rocks, along with the smaller ones, the stones. All must be dealt with in order to clear the road for us to travel forward. Why should we do this? Because we are His people, and He has chosen us. He promises us freedom from everything that has served to hold us captive in the past.

I encourage you to take this seventh step. *"Please, God, take it away. I'm tired of dealing with all this stuff. I can't do it in my own strength, I need Your help."* That can be the cry of your heart in this step. We come before God in humility and ask Him to take away what we cannot remove ourselves. And then we lean on our convictions and readiness from the last step we took. Openness, trust, and patience. Open to allowing God to be the architect, not ourselves. Trusting that He is capable and faithful to complete the work in our lives. Patient in our efforts to simply take it one step at a time as He puts things in front of us. And then we walk humbly forward, with the recognition that perhaps God knows best.

Prayer

Heavenly Father, You designed us before the universe was even created. You have plans for our lives, plans to prosper and bless us.

We live in a fallen world, some things beyond our control and some things of our own making. Please remove our shortcomings and help us to move beyond them into the plans You have for us. Amen.

Questions

1. When I look at what motivates my actions, who am I serving?

2. Am I ready to walk forward in this new direction? What is He calling me to step into today?

3. Is there any obstacle in my path that I need to clear away with His help so I can move forward?

Chapter 8
Embrace the Journey

We're all on a journey together on this little ball of mud and water called Earth. A journey to understand what we've been put here for, where we've come from, and where we're going. We've been looking to scripture and, in particular, the story of the prodigal son as a road map for our journey thus far. Here's a "Coles Notes" version of the story to refresh us:

1. One of two sons demands his inheritance early from his father, then runs off and squanders it on wild living.
2. He returns to his senses and plans to work for the family as a hired hand.
3. His father forgives and restores him however, while his brother refuses to.

That's the overall story from which we'll look into more detail as we go through this step. In the last chapter, we humbly asked God to remove our shortcomings and now we're ready to start turning outwards as we continue to move forward. Step 8 reads:

"Made a list of all persons we had harmed, and became willing to make amends to them all."

"Made a list of all persons we had harmed...". That doesn't sound that hard. Get out our paper and pencil and start listing things we've done, hurts we've caused, etc. Wait a minute, didn't we already do this though? In step four, we "made a searching and fearless moral inventory of ourselves." Didn't we deal with and move past this stuff? Isn't it all in the rearview mirror? We need to remember that this is a journey we're on, a journey of restoration. Steps 4 and 5 were about looking at ourselves, the nature of our wrongs, and how our actions have harmed others. Step 5 was about achieving some restoration through confession and forgiveness. That part of our journey focused on our relationship with God, ourselves and the rest of humanity. It aimed to deal with our sense of separateness and alienation from the physical and spiritual world. This step is about building on that work and starting the restoration process with the other individuals in our lives.

Now, before we go on, I want to stop and encourage you for a second. When we're on this journey, it can begin to seem like a pretty long one. It's a lot of work, and there always seems to be more to do, another step to take. Are we ever going to arrive? The simple answer is no, not this side of heaven. However, I still want to encourage us to take heart and continue because it gets easier. If we need to stop and sit on a bench along the way, that's perfectly fine. Life isn't meant to be a sprint. We need to pace ourselves and continue when we're ready. The most important part of the race is our desire to stay in it, so I encourage you to do so.

The step eight is about laying the groundwork for our journey forward for the rest of our lives. Have you ever tackled something big? (I don't mean tackling that one giant friend we all seem to have). Ever built something or, say, started university? Nothing happens overnight. Building something, you need to plan, prepare, lay the foundation, and then build on each step as it comes. Heading off to school, you have introductory courses your freshman year, and you start to focus your studies the second year. Each year after that builds on the previous one. Doctors take at least 7 years of schooling and then spend another couple in practical residency. That takes a lot of commitment. But ask yourself, would you want someone operating on you who just started biology 101 last month?

This journey we're on is no different. It will take some commitment on our part to keep moving forward, to grow, and to deal with the stuff that traps us in the past. If it seems that we're not making progress, that the journey is slow, that's alright. We need to keep our eyes on the goal, placing one foot in front of the other and taking the next step.

In the last chapter, we talked about needing to be open, trusting, and patient. To be open to allowing God to be the architect, not ourselves. Trusting that He is capable and faithful to complete the work in our lives. Patient in our efforts to simply take it one step at a time as He puts things in front of us. Like me, I suspect that you always want to jump to the end and know what it will look like. There's something I find myself saying over and over to people I meet with and counsel. (I often have to take my own advice and remind myself as well of this question) If you will, imagine an elephant on a big (on a massive) platter in front of you, all roasted, with a giant apple in its mouth like a roast pig, and someone says that you need to eat it. What do you do? How do you eat a whole elephant? You pick up your fork and knife and begin *one bite at a time*. That's how you eat an elephant. That's how we continue on this life journey, one step at a time, not worrying about and perhaps paralyzing ourselves by trying to see the end of the path.

So, back to this "list." Who do we include on this list? Anyone we've harmed in some way. I'll get into more detail in a minute about what we should consider as "harm," but we need to include anyone we've harmed in this list in some way. Anyone. I'll repeat it, *anyone*.

Now, that might seem a bit daunting or even frightening when we start to think about it. Anyone. Everyone. Everyone I've hurt in some way? What about if they've harmed me? Do they count, then? The second part of this step talks about amends. What about if they don't even know about what I've done? Do I need to include those as well? We need to remember that this step is all about making the list, not taking action on the list. So be thorough. Anyone. If we've done something to someone, include it. We'll sort out what to do next later; that's not the concern right now.

So what do we mean by "harm"? That can and will be quite varied. Physical harms — have we actually hit or injured others in some way? Have we stolen from others? Have we not followed through on our financial commitments and left others picking up the pieces? Emotional harms — have we verbally abused others and tore down their sense of worth and belonging? Have we removed ourselves from other's lives through our actions, leaving them feeling cheated or abandoned? Spiritual harms — have we judged others and caused them to question their faith? Have we led others in our care not to recognize and develop their spiritual relationships? Now, the list can go on and on. These are just a few examples of what harm can be. We need to consider our lives and come up with our own list.

As with all things, I encourage you to take on this task first by bathing it in prayer. Ask God to open your eyes to the harm you've caused, both intentional and unintentional. Sometimes, we've done things that we didn't even mean to or know that we've done. Ask Him to help you see the connections and own your part.

A word of advice when you undertake this exercise: be as objective as you can, and don't give in to the power of emotion. Worrying about including something on your list that will require dealing with immediately will drag you off course and stall your progress. The whole point of this exercise is to compile a list so you can identify the issues and then look to address them appropriately. The second part of this step, "becoming willing," doesn't mean we must act on each case. Our next step will address who and when. In this step, we need to be willing to look at each case of our actions, study, recognize our part, and list them down. We're looking to get them out so we can objectively look at them and not let them drive us anymore. Doing so allows us the freedom to move in a new direction. Loneliness and isolation are often where we live, trapped by shame and guilt over past actions. This step is the start of addressing that by preparing us to restore relationships with those around us, those we bump up against each day. The idea of that can be frightening, but again, I encourage you to take this one step at a time, trusting that He will lead you forward when you're ready.

Earlier in looking at who to include in our list, the question came up about including those who've harmed us. If we decide to go down that road justifying our actions based on other's actions and not including them on our list, we're falling for a very deadly trap. We need to own our parts and list them.

Perhaps even more importantly, we need to seek to forgive others who have harmed us. Why? For a number of reasons, actually. One is that it helps us to understand more fully what we will ask of others. If we strive to make amends and ask for forgiveness from others for our actions, how can we not hold out the same offer? We must freely offer forgiveness if we do not want to remain trapped in our pasts. I want to point out something here that there is often confusion about. Forgiveness does not necessarily mean forgetting and continuing as if nothing has ever happened. Forgiveness is not about blindly proceeding forward and not utilizing wisdom to guide our actions in the future. Forgiveness is actually about placing the issue, or a better term would be *returning* it to where it truly belongs, with the perpetrator, not the victim. We cannot change the actions of another person, so why would we want to stay captive to them? Why would we want to carry around that baggage with us? It just gets heavier and heavier, so again, I encourage you to forgive others and pass the bag back to them to deal with.

With that in mind, I want to turn now to the story of the prodigal son to see what it can tell us about this eighth step we're on. There are actually two things we can learn; one demonstrates and points to the benefit of taking this step, while the other highlights the danger of refusing to. I'm sure more things can be learned as well; I am not trying to say that I have found the only nuggets in this story. So when you get the chance, reread the story for yourself and see what jumps out at you. I bet you'll be amazed at how it comes to life.

If we recall the story from earlier, the prodigal son had demanded his inheritance early and ran off, wasting it in a far-off land. Out of money and starving, in verse 18, we're told he decides to take some action. In essence, he takes the eighth step. In Luke chapter 15, verse 18, we read:

"I will go home to my father and say 'Father, I have sinned against both heaven and you,'".

"I have sinned"; that's another way of saying I have harmed, isn't it? And who has he harmed? His father and God. How does he know that? Why would he identify both of those parties? He's looked back at his actions and considered how they have affected others. He's reviewed, identified, and made a list of his transgressions. There you have it - step 8! And now he plans to head

home and make amends.

So what were his sins or harms? While not a comprehensive list, they can serve as stepping stones to possibly identify our own harms I believe. I'm sure he dishonored his father and caused some emotional harm in v 12 by demanding his inheritance early. He lusted after his father's belongings rather than cherishing the relationship that was being offered to him. Now, we've never done that before... have we? We've never based how much time we give someone, our willingness to engage in a relationship based on their social and financial status... have we? We've never looked at the car or bike and failed to even take a second glance at the one driving ...have we?

The son we're told in the story wasted his money on "wild living." His brother fills in more detail later when he says that his brother wasted his inheritance on prostitutes. We can assume that along with that, such a lifestyle probably included alcohol and partying. We've never engaged in such things, have we? Gotten drunk and smoked some dope? Perhaps not employing a prostitute, but how about engaging in risky sex? Been there, done that, got the shirt.

This story does not provide us with a comprehensive list of what to look for when creating our own lists. However, isn't it amazing how something written 2000 years ago, details the cares and concerns of today just like it was written yesterday? That is the power of the living Word. This story can speak and help us identify issues in our own lives and encourage us in our walk along this journey.

The son decided to do step 8, identify his sins, and was willing to try to make amends. His willingness did not guarantee that relationships would be restored. In fact, he thought that he was headed home to become a servant. Isn't it amazing though, how his willingness is what put him in a place where there was possibility of restoration to occur? Unless he'd been *willing* and taken the step, there could have been no different future. So take heart, take this step, and who knows what the next step will bring!

Now, the second piece we need to look at in this story is the brother who stayed home. The brother in this story we remember refused to forgive. Coming home from work one night, he finds a party taking place, celebrating his brother's return. Verse 28 tells us that *"The older brother was angry and wouldn't go in."* Now, did he have the right to be angry with his brother? Yes. Anger in and of itself is not a sin. Jesus Himself we're told, got angry. Angry at the money changers in the temple for ripping people off and not honoring God.

Anger can be righteous. To be righteous means to be in the right relationship with God. So, we are called to righteous anger when confronted with something that is not in the right relationship with God. We are right to be angry with things that don't line up with His character, such as abuse, poverty, and sexual exploitation, to name a few examples.

The brother's anger was justified because his brother had harmed him, his father, and God he had broken their relationship.

What we do in our anger is where we get into trouble, and that is the case here with the brother. He refuses to forgive, and his refusal traps him into hanging onto the past. His anger leads him into sin when he disrespects his father by refusing to follow his example and ignoring his father's pleading to come and join the celebration. He begins to look inward and become selfish. He points to the fact that their father had given the brother his inheritance early and now throws a party. He complains about killing the fattened calf while he has never been given anything for staying home and serving. Now, who is coveting in this story?

Remember I said that we need to engage each of these steps everyday of our lives? This is exactly a case in point. The brother had the right to be angry. But, when faced with the choice of what to do in his anger, he steps off the path and isn't willing to engage in step 8. If he had taken the time to assess the situation, he may have recognized his sin. Then, if willing to make amends, he wouldn't have missed the boat. Instead, he is trapped, held captive, and driven by his sin. And where do we find those like him? Outside the party. Outside of life as it's been designed and meant to be lived. Living in broken relationships with little hope for anything different in the future. That is the real and present danger of refusal to engage in this journey.

So, in conclusion, I've said all along that this is a journey of restoration. If something needs to be restored, by definition, it is not all that it formerly was or can be. So, I've been encouraging you and will continue to encourage you to have courage and commit to taking the next step as it presents itself. I believe each of these steps is something we must be doing all the time in our everyday life and I'm excited at the prospect of the future. We're all on a journey together on this little ball of mud and water called Earth. A journey to understand what we've been put here for, where we've come from, and where we're going. I hope that as we walk together, we can enjoy each other's company and learn from one another along the way.

Prayer

Heavenly Father, please give us insight to see and recognize when we've harmed others in our past. Shine a light that we may see through Your eyes to make our list and help us to be willing to make amends wherever they may be. Thank You, Jesus. Amen.

Questions

1. Are you committed to continuing this journey? Do you believe that He has a future worth walking into for you?

2. Do you find you can justify any of your actions based on the actions of others? Is there anyone you need to forgive to move ahead on your journey?

3. Pen to paper time. Who have I harmed with my actions/inactions/ words etc?

"Hey Pig, Keep the Slop. I'm Going Home!"

Chapter 9
I'm Sorry...

Only three more to go after this one! This journey has covered a lot of ground. We've moved from recognizing that we have a control problem to living in such a way that by giving up control, we actually gain it. As we build on the last step we took, we look to begin restoring some broken relationships in our lives. I would like to pause for a moment. Remember, this is a journey that we're on. It's not a race, or at least not a sprint, but a marathon. We simply need to continue putting one foot in front of the other to make progress. The journey of restored lives is not for the faint of heart; it is a challenge that is picked up and embraced. The rewards, I assure you, are worth it because they mean life itself!

So, let's take the next step. Step 9 reads:

"We made direct amends to such people wherever possible, except when to do so would injure them or others."

Make direct amends...to whom and for what? Well, if you recall the last step you took, you compiled a list of all those whom you'd harmed. Harmed through lying, cheating, stealing, you name it. We each have a list of people our past actions have harmed. The specifics look different, but the underlying issues and actions fall into the same camp. They've all led to broken relationships in some way.

So, in this step, we're going to try to address some of our actions. We're going to seek out those we've harmed, apologize, and make up for it where we can. Easy peasy, right? By lunchtime tomorrow, we'll be all caught up and ready to move onward, NOT! If we're truly honest, do we look at the task ahead with just a little fear in our hearts? This step is a challenging one, not for the faint of heart. But, if we want to continue this restoration journey, we must set ourselves to this task and continue to push ahead. I'll speak in a bit about the dangers of not doing so, but first, I want us to explore what is at the heart of this step in our journey. What is it trying to accomplish truly?

Why do we make amends with people, and what exactly are amends anyways? Amends can look very different based on the circumstances, but essentially, they are a making right of something. They can be setting the story straight when we've engaged in deceit. They can pay back debts when we default on them. They can be returning what doesn't belong to us when we've stolen or cheated. They can be following through on a promise we've made but didn't before. As you can see, amends can be as varied as the situations you've found yourself in. At the heart of them, though, whatever they may look like, is a desire to restore the relationship that has been broken. That is one of the main reasons we do them. The other, which is why it is being addressed so late in our journey, has to do with our hearts. We're on step nine of a twelve-step journey, three-quarters of the way there. We thought we were on the homeward stretch, didn't we? This step offers us one of our greatest challenges so far and is crucial if we are going to have any hope of living on a different path than before. Accepting this challenge is central to joy and peace in our future. To fail to engage will lead to a future burdened with the pain and turmoil of living, as the saying goes, as a "dry drunk."

Our heart. What does our heart have to do with this step? Well, up to this point in our journey, I would suggest that, primarily, our actions have been self-focused or motivated. We've become tired of living with the consequences of our decisions and actions. We've recognized that we cannot do this alone and need God's help, but that decision was ultimately self-motivated, wasn't it? Turning our lives over was done because we wanted something better for ourselves than we had before. Now, I'm not saying that is wrong. The steps we've taken so far lead to the only way we have hope for a future.

Again, I'm just trying to point out that we're on a journey. And like any journey, there will be pieces to deal with as we get to them at their appropriate time. As I'm writing this, we still have a bit of snow outside, and the temperatures are close to the freezing mark. As I look out my window, I see that the weather here in

Kelowna is nothing compared to the cold we moved from in Winnipeg. Brrrr! Sorry, Winnipegers. I'm glad we made the move! As I stop and recall those cold days, the weather serves as a good analogy for where we're at in this journey. Maybe you live where you need to plug your car in overnight or have heard of such a place. In Winnipeg, however, you absolutely need to if you want your car to start the next morning. So, the night before you want to go somewhere, you need to prepare and take a step. You plug in the car's block heater in order to start the car the next day. Then, once you've fired up the car, you need to let it sit and warm up a bit. This gets the oil circulating and the whole engine up to temperature before you shift it into gear and drive away. If you don't take that step, you risk blowing the motor and stopping the planned journey!

This step nine we're starting to tackle today is just like that. It couldn't have been done any sooner because it relies on the work done in the previous steps to set it up for success. So this brings us back to our heart. You might say that our heart has been self-absorbed up to this point in our journey. We've taken steps to reach out and embrace God and humanity as a whole to restore those relationships. The heart of those decisions has been inwardly focused, and they've been made with an eye to our own benefit. And they needed to be. Only by taking those actions so far have we done the work that has allowed us to become healthy enough to take this next step.

In step nine, God is reaching into us and molding a new heart. An outward-focused heart. One that strives to understand, share, and be guided by the feelings of another (to be empathetic). A heart that looks to benefit others even before ourselves. We benefit from taking this step, don't get me wrong. Step nine is not all about self-sacrifice and being a martyr, so don't hear me say that. In this part of our journey, God seeks to transform us more and more into His image, His character. He turns our eyes from self to others, and we begin to perceive the world in a whole new light. We begin to move from being "takers" to becoming "givers" of life.

Have you ever given someone a gift you knew they would be absolutely thrilled about? You put a lot of thought into ensuring it was just right. Something that, once given, you knew would be cherished by the receiver. Why do we do that? Are we looking for a gift in return? Is it a scratch my back, and I'll scratch your type of equation? No, I would submit that we give such gifts because we want to give joy to someone else. We want them to be happy. The heart in such giving is not self-motivated but is outward-focused. The funny thing is, though, that the giving richly blesses us. Something deep in us is nourished and built up when we focus on someone else, isn't it? You see, that's the step we're ready to take now.

Step nine *is* about restoring relationships, but even more so about changing our hearts to be one of a servant, outward focused, and set up for success in our lives to come. This life we live as followers of Christ is all about becoming more and more transformed into His likeness. We are to become more and more like Him. And who was He, what was He like? Well, He came as a servant, looking to restore and bless us. He even put His life on the line, giving us the ultimate gift of life through His death on the cross. So, in step nine, we are simply living out the mandate that He has called us to as His followers.

If we consider ourselves Christians, we don't really have a choice but to take up this challenge, do we? This is exactly the life journey that He's called us to. This is part of why I chose to call this journey "Life Steps" rather than "12 steps of something...". Often, as people who do not struggle with identified addictions like alcohol and drugs, gambling or eating, etc, we set ourselves apart from those people. We aren't them, so we don't need to apply these steps to our own lives. Well, as we can see, the wisdom found in the scriptures is just as applicable to those outside traditional 12-step circles as those within them. Whatever your struggle, the whole point of the steps is to lead to a transformed life. A life where we live as we're meant to live, in the right relationship with each other and with God. We need to remember that these steps, compiled by AA founders, were drawn from the Bible. They are simply His principles for life; hence, they are "Life Steps"!

Now, we can look at some practical aspects of this step, and that's where the story of the prodigal son can help us. Do you remember where we found that story? Lk 15:11-31. If we remember, the prodigal son found himself in a far-off land, starving to death after wasting his inheritance on wild living. We just looked at how he "came to his senses," as the text says, and did a step eight. He stopped and thought about how he'd harmed his father and God and became willing to make amends by deciding that he should head home to seek forgiveness. This is where we pick up the story in verse 20:

"So he got up and went to his father. "But while he was still a long way off, his father saw him and was filled with compassion for him; he ran to his son, threw his arms around him and kissed him. "The son said to him, 'Father, I have sinned against heaven and against you. I am no longer worthy to be called your son.'" ~ Luke 15:20, 21 NIV

The prodigal son decided to take up the challenge of step nine, didn't he? We're told that he put his plan into action and returned to his father. Now, in your own step nine, you may also be called to do so. You may have to pick up the phone, write a letter, get in your car, and make contact with someone on your list from step eight. I asked earlier if we approach this step with just a little fear in our hearts. Our fears are justified and natural. In fact, if we do not have at least a little hesitancy in our hearts, I'd question how thorough our step eight list has been. Perhaps we haven't really scraped more than the surface of our actions and harms. Our fears are justified and natural, as attempts at making amends with people may not go as we hope. They may not be open to forgiving and restoring relationships. My point is that brokenness is guaranteed to continue unless you take this step. So, what do you really have to lose?

In the story of the prodigal son, the son's hopes are far surpassed by his father's love and desire to restore their relationship. This is an example of the best-case scenario for making amends. However, it is also pretty demonstrative of the heart of most of those we are going to be reaching out to. I believe you will be pleasantly surprised at the acceptance and forgiveness offered by those you make amends to. Most of the time, when people see that we are trying to be genuine and we're really making an honest effort to live differently, they are willing to meet us more than halfway because they want to support and see us succeed. We need to remember that we, humanity, have been made in His image and that He desires community. We shouldn't be surprised when we are drawn toward restoration rather than breaking a relationship.

What about situations where we can't make amends? Perhaps we don't know where the person we've harmed is, they've moved away, or maybe they've even passed on. In these cases, and it varies with each unique situation, I'd recommend either writing a letter out or sitting down and making amends to God as a surrogate. Actually, engaging in the amends is the point of these cases. There won't be a restoration of the physical relationship. However, by taking this step, we will help accomplish the goal of changing our hearts to desire restoration and demonstrate to ourselves that we are willing and capable of doing so. This leads us to another situation where making amends is perhaps not appropriate at this time.

In this step, we're called to make amends where possible unless doing so would harm others. Well, what does that mean exactly? There is a quote from the AA Big Book that I really like, and I believe it truly sums up the heart of the matter. "*We must remember that we cannot buy our peace of mind at the expense of others."* [4] The harm you've done in the past has certainly not always been done in isolation. You may have had "partners in crime," so to speak. Naming them could cause grief to them or their relationships. Or you may have done things that, if brought to light too quickly or unwisely, may endanger your loved ones, your job, or your home. Sometimes, your amends have to wait until an appropriate time and place. Your piece of the amends process, at this time, will be to carry the burden of it for now simply. I'm not saying to carry the guilt of it; we dealt with that back in step five and have been forgiven. However, we may have to live without resolution for a while until God opens up an opportunity to deal with an issue. This leads us to the other side of the coin when dealing with amends. While sometimes we may have to wait because taking action would cause more harm, we also have to watch that we are not using such concerns as an excuse not to act. There is another quote that I like from the Big Book; *"Let's not talk prudence while practicing evasion."* [5]

This whole step and amends process must be bathed in prayer, asking for wisdom, timing, and opportunities from God to make amends when appropriate. This is an ongoing process; there may be harms that we've forgotten about and amends that have not been made. We also need to keep this in prayer, asking that God help us keep an open mind to recall those we've forgotten to make amends to.

"Hey Pig, Keep the Slop. I'm Going Home!"

The final piece I'd like to look at, and we touched on the last step as well, is the danger if we do not take up the challenge of this step. The prodigal son's brother had been faithful and stayed home working on the farm, serving his father. At the end of the story, though, he finds himself standing outside the house, angry and alone. This older brother is a picture of what life looks like when we don't stay committed to the path. As hard as the step in front of us looks, he demonstrates the outcome when we don't accept the challenge to take it. He had a right to be angry with his brother. If the story were to include a conversation between the two brothers, we'd probably get a good example of how an attempted amendment will not always go well. But we're not given that. What we are given in the story is instead a picture of how the brother is actually inward-focused. He is caught up in a sense of entitlement, thinking about how he has been faithful, yet his father has not met his needs. The older brother has not embraced step nine, allowing God to change his focus outward. By doing so, he allows God to mold in him a new empathetic heart, one that seeks to serve and restore his relationship with his brother. The decision to turn inward leaves him angry and alone outside the party, outside life. Let this example burn itself into our hearts and minds as we go forward in our journeys. As we make amends to those we've harmed and respond to those who desire to make amends with us, I pray that we accept the challenge put to us in this step. Let us truly become His image bearers and live out the promise of a baby boy who came into the world to change it forever.

Prayer

Heavenly Father, thank You for walking side by side with us as we make amends where we can. Mold in us a new heart that seeks to serve rather than be served. Thank You, Jesus. Amen.

Questions

1. Are you ready to start this part of your journey? Are you ready to move from being a "taker" to a "giver" of life? What about that excites you?

2. Pick something from your Step 8 list and plan to address it. Why did you pick this item?

3. After picking the "cherries" (the easy items) on your list, look at those remaining. Are there some that you're talking about prudence while actually practicing evasion?

Chapter 10
What's Up Doc?

We've been on this restoration journey for a while now and are nearing the end finally. Or are we? As this chapter will point out, this journey is actually the one that serves us to continue to take to heart each day for the rest of the time given to us. That being said, though, don't be dismayed; this book will end in a couple of chapters. I'm sure that will make some readers happy!

So, step 10, and we're off!

"We continued to take personal inventory and, when we were wrong, promptly admitted it."

We continued to take personal inventory .if you remember back in step 4, we looked back at our lives and made a list of all the persons we had wronged. The following steps helped us to deal with those issues and put them behind us. We asked and received forgiveness from God for those things. In the last few steps, we have even asked and sometimes received forgiveness from some of the people directly that we harmed. That stuff is behind us, and this step is not trying to deal with our previous inventory. This is a completely new step. Like a regular visit to the doctor, you don't deal with old, healed surgeries and broken bones. You are simply there for a checkup, looking for any new issues that have arisen.

I just draw us back to step 4 so we can remember what it was that we were doing what we were inventorying. In that step, we looked at how the prodigal son came to his senses and recognized the sins that he had committed against his father, God, and even himself. We said that in looking at ourselves, we need some way of identifying the things that we'd done wrong. The prodigal son says that he has "sinned", so that was the term we decided to use as a guide. We then looked at a list of the seven deadly sins, so we had some criteria or categories from which to start an inspection of our actions. The seven deadly sins we found out are pride, greed, lust, anger, gluttony, envy, and sloth. We can use the same list as our jump-off point in this step.

So now I want to look at three things about doing a daily personal inventory. The first is why. Why must we do an inventory again if we handled this six steps ago? Let's do a little exercise that will, I hope, make a point. If it doesn't, well, at least we'll be more relaxed. Stop what you're doing and take a deep breath - in through your nose and breathe out through your mouth. And again, in through the nose, out through the mouth. Excellent. Did you feel your lungs fill up? Feel that sense of movement as your chest expands and contracts as you breathe in and out. Good. You know what that means? You're alive. Isn't that amazing?! Quite the revelation, Brad! Thanks, Captain Obvious.

Seriously though, do you know what else that means? We each have a new list, a new inventory. As long as our chest rises and falls, we continue to make bad decisions and act on them. We continue to "sin". Perhaps you've had to deal with busy traffic or crowded malls and maybe didn't think the nicest thoughts about the person who cut you off. Or how about the salesperson who seemed to serve everyone else first? Come on, be honest. I'll admit that I have thought it would be good to have a big brush guard bumper on my vehicle sometimes. Just because that other driver really deserved to be put into the wall. I had to stop and ask forgiveness for that while I was writing this.

Now, I'm not saying that everything we do is bad; don't hear me say that. I'm just pointing out that we are fallen people living in a fallen world. We *will keep falling despite* our good intentions, and that's just a fact of life. This step, however, helps us to address that tendency. Hopefully, it helps reduce it as we develop new habits and ways of dealing with things - as we're gradually *restored* to how things were originally designed.

So we know we need to do this step because we each still have an inventory to list, and that list grows every day. But the bigger question is, why must we deal with these things? Let bygones be bygones, and simply continue trying to do better next time. Now tell me, did you ever spill something, your coffee or dinner on the way to the table? How about your popcorn on the way to your seat at the movie? That one is real upsetting, considering the ridiculous price of theatre snacks. Well, in all those situations, we could simply continue resolving to avoid doing that again. That doesn't really help to restore things, though. That doesn't clean the floor so we don't slip and repeat the accident the next time we go that way. That doesn't help those around us to not slip themselves either, does it? When we don't own our part of a mess and help deal with it, a message is sent to those around us impacted by it that they are perhaps not important enough to warrant action. That we have bigger and better things to deal with. How do those types of thoughts affect those relationships? How do those kinds of thoughts impact *our* thoughts in the future? What habits do *we* develop? You can see, and I don't believe this to be a great revelation to us, that we need to address things when we do them wrong. If we don't, they tend to repeat themselves and have a greater and greater negative impact on our lives. Just like spilling stuff and not cleaning up, eventually, we live in a pig pen, and who wants to live there? By dealing with things in a timely manner, we keep our accounts short. Doing so serves those we've hurt and helps us not be burdened by them, becoming triggered into old behaviours as the weight becomes unbearable.

If we choose not to address things promptly and continue in life, our "baggage" from the previous day carries over into the next. We may even admit to ourselves at the time that we blew it over something and recognize that we need to deal with it at some point in the future. We continue to the next day and the next. What happens as we continue, adding to our pile of undealt issues each day? Where are our eyes drawn, and what gains our attention? The most recent transgression, right? As we have more and more issues, hurts, etc, to deal with, we kind of go into firefighting mode. We focus on the latest hotspot to flare up, trying to get through it so we can survive yet another day.

What happens to the previous issues? When do we look at them? Short answer: we don't. The current issue has our attention riveted on it as we try to balance our lives, even though the task becomes more and more unmanageable. Where have we heard that before? And what happens eventually? Crash! Like a house of cards, everything falls down. What are we left with? All the same issues. Except now they've had the chance to grow. What was a simple spilled coffee, a simple clean-up job, has now turned into a stain on the carpet. That unintended snub has now developed into full-blown hostility and a relationship breakdown. Anger, when not dealt with promptly and left to fester and grow, turns into bitterness and resentment. They are a whole different thing compared to anger. They permeate everything, infecting stuff that wasn't even bad. This is exactly why we need to engage in step 10 on a *daily* basis, assessing our lives and taking action to clean up the mess as it happens.

So, what is it that we need to be looking out for? This is the second thing I want to look at. What should we be identifying in our inventory? Remember the list we used last time. Pride, greed, lust, anger, gluttony, envy and sloth. Those are good places to start. Another would be to simply ask ourselves these types of questions:

"Am I doing to others as I would have them do to me - today?"

Was there a time today that I acted out of pride? How did that affect those around me? Would I have wanted to be in their shoes?

Did I look at what someone had today and want it for my own?

Did I let someone get under my skin and speak harshly to them? Or perhaps ignored them entirely just to make a point? Did that serve to build or break our relationship?

Was there a job at work today that needed to be done, but I ducked because I really didn't feel like doing it? What extra burden did that put on the rest of the team?

All of these things are examples of what to keep an eye out for as we do our own inventory. I'm sure you can add a great number of things to the list.

Most things are pretty obvious when we think about them. However, some things can be tricky, especially when we factor in our tendency to self-deceive. Some of our daily actions are done for specific reasons: to move somebody or point out something. There are motives behind a lot of our decisions and actions. That's perfectly legitimate; we can do things because we're motivated to help someone. We need to look at not only our actions, however, but our motivations as well as we compile our inventory. This is where we need to specifically be on guard against our ability to self-deceive. We can justify almost all of our actions if we really want to, but that doesn't mean they are all justified. Consider things such as:

Was that really meant as constructive criticism, or were we

really trying to win an argument?

Were we trying to teach a lesson, or were we looking to punish?

What was motivating our decisions and actions? Was there pride, fear, or jealousy lurking in the background? How about anger or anxiousness?

So in our step 10 inventory, we need to not only consider our actions but also why we took action. When one of those things doesn't line up with what we would have done to ourselves, write it down.

The third and final thing I want to explore is how. How do we practically do step 10? What does that look like? It's all fine and dandy to say that we need to consider our actions daily and address them. It's just a lot of ungraspable smoke without some concrete boots on the ground direction, though, isn't it?

Pick a time. A lot of people will choose bedtime as they lay their heads on their pillows and get ready to go to sleep. That may or may not work for you. Whatever time you pick, it doesn't matter. What does matter is that you pick a time and stick with it. Many people will say that their time is fluid, and they seize opportunities throughout the day as they present themselves. A free five minutes here, a quiet lunchtime there. That's fine, and I encourage taking these times to act. However, I would also strongly encourage you to pick a designated time each day and commit to it along with these extra times. Why? Because a set time promotes habit forming and continued practice. A time that moves around lends itself to being squeezed out of our schedule as a day sometimes seems to run itself. Ever look at the clock and be amazed that it's that late already?

So pick a time and then consider your day. Step through it: what's happened, your conversations, your thoughts, your motivations, your actions. And don't just look for the "bad" things! Step 10 is *not* meant to be an exercise in drudgery, where we look with an eye to beat ourselves up. Look for the good things that happened in your day as well. Look at your actions, words, and thoughts that lifted others and yourself up. Identify and celebrate those good things just as much as you look for places you could have handled better. When you find those things that you could have done better, simply think them through a bit. How could you have handled them better? What could've been done differently? Maybe you need to make something right the next day or make an apology. Then, commit to trying harder *next* time and ask God for help. Notice I said commit to trying harder *next* time. There will be a next time.

We may blow it again, but as we try harder each time, the right way becomes easier. You will eventually find yourself handling it better the next time it comes up. So tell me, have you ever served in the armed forces? How about played a sport on a regular basis? Consider what soldiers do in boot camp - drills. There's one thing all athletes do to get better at their game - practise. Why do these people do these things? To get better, yes, but how does it make them better? As they practise, the moves become instinctual, and they don't need to devote conscious thought to do them. They just naturally move that way and accomplish their goal. Did they start out that way? No. The green recruit didn't have the faintest idea how to march or shoot his rifle. That pitcher had no idea how to hold the ball and whip his arm. Over time, those things became natural to them. They can then focus their attention on where they placed the bullet or the ball, couldn't they? Step 10 is no different. As we develop a rhythm of looking at our day, making amends, and striving to do better the next time, we also learn to naturally handle things differently and better. Then, we can move our focus to the next task at hand.

In concluding our look at step 10, I want to encourage you to keep in mind God's desire for you as written in 1 John:

"If we claim we have no sin, we are only fooling ourselves and not living in the truth. But if we confess our sins to Him, He is faithful and just to forgive us our sins and to cleanse us from all wickedness." ~ 1 John 1:8-9

So, as you go through each day and take the time to look back and address it's issues, He is faithful to wipe the slate clean again. As you continue that rhythm, life remains manageable. You're able to focus your attention on what needs to be done to build and grow relationships with those around you and with God. You become evermore restored to what was meant to be in the first place.

Prayer

Heavenly Father, thank you for designing me to grow to learn new ways of living. Help me to look daily at my thoughts/actions/motivations and build new muscles of life and hope. Thank You, Jesus. Amen.

Questions

1. When am I going to do this step? What time works for me to set aside daily to stop and consider the last 24 hours?

2. What could I have done better today? Why did I do it that way? What was my motivation? Are there any amends I need to make?

3. What went well today? What did I handle differently, better than I have in the past? How does that make me feel?

Chapter 11
So Tell Me About Yourself...

We've reached the 11th step in our journey of restoration! Step 11 reads:

"Sought through prayer and meditation to improve our conscious contacts with God as we understood Him, praying only for the knowledge of His will for us and the power to carry that out."

Before we dig into it, though, let's take a quick glance at the road we've travelled so far. Retracing how He has been faithful will help us as we exercise our own faith in this current step by reaching out to God.

Can you name the biblical story that we've been looking at so far and where it is found? (I hope so, or my prodding thus far has been for nought!) The story of the Prodigal Son is found in the Gospel of Luke, Chapter 15, verses 11 through 31. These twenty verses weave quite the tale. A boy demands his inheritance early, runs off, squanders it, and then realizes his bad decisions. He comes home looking to become a hired servant, but his father, in an amazing picture of grace, restores him. Definitely a picture of our story and our Heavenly Father.

So in our journey, as we've taken each step so far, we, like the prodigal son, have recognized that if left to our own devices, we blow it. We need guidance and help and have come to realize that there exists a loving God who wants to help us if we just ask and let Him. He has walked with us each step of the way as we've examined our past, admitted, and turned it over. Under His direction, our footing has been solid as we've tried to make up where we could and as we've left what we couldn't in His care.

In step 10, we decided that we needed to stay on top of our amends. Doing so allows us to deal with them directly before they build up and lead back into a life that becomes unmanageable. We decided that we needed to examine our day daily, didn't we? To look at it frankly, not to beat ourselves up, but to look at how we can make things right and do better next time. At this point in our journey, we're now really striving to live in the solution. We've dealt with our past and put it behind us. And so we are here, looking to take this eleventh step. Are you ready? Step 11 reads:

"Sought through prayer and meditation to improve our conscious contacts with God as we understood Him, praying only for the knowledge of His will for us and the power to carry that out."

So this is really about continuing to move forward in this

new life, isn't it? The language of this step is all about movement, about the passage of time - our living in the solution. Conscious contacts - multiple, ongoing. Praying for knowledge of His will and then carrying it out - doing something and then moving forward in action.

Steps 10 through 12 are sometimes called the "maintenance steps," which perhaps has a bit of a negative connotation to it. Maintenance, that's what we do with our cars, our houses, the gym, sounds a bit like dreary work doesn't it? We need to keep in mind the point of maintenance though, to keep something running. To keep it useful and moving. An unmaintained car eventually dies. A maintained one will keep you moving as you need, taking you to new destinations and new adventures! So it is with these last three steps doing this work keeps us moving forward and remaining healthy. We're then able to experience this new restored life we've been called into.

Step 11 - *"Sought through prayer and meditation to improve our conscious contacts with God as we understood Him, praying only for the knowledge of His will for us and the power to carry that out."* That's a bit of a mouthful, but what exactly does it mean? I want to explore a couple of things. First, why would we do this? What are we trying to accomplish? And secondly how, what does this step look like practically, and how do we walk it out?

So first, why *"Improve our conscious contacts with God"*? Why would we want to do that? I guess in my mind, I'm asking the question, why wouldn't we want to do that? But for anyone who has only recently made a connection with our Heavenly Father, this can seem like a bit of a daunting task. *Me*, little ol me, spend time with the creator of the universe? The simplest explanation of why we do this would be to point to any relationship you have. Why would we want to increase our contact with someone? Perhaps to get to know them more. To gain some insight into what motivates and drives them. It's hard to develop a relationship without connecting time, right? Note the difference in your relationships between Facebook friends and real people that you interact with on a daily or weekly basis. The people you see and touch every day, you have a greater understanding and a deeper connection to. Facebook is a great connecting tool, but it doesn't generally give us depth in our relationships. I think at last count, there are over 1000 friends listed in my Facebook account. That's great and I enjoy getting to see updates on their lives. But we don't have deep relationships that shape our lives or influence our daily decisions. There are not enough hours in the day to have a deep relationship with each of these people. The distances that would need to be travelled alone would be an insurmountable barrier. I'd be the airline's favorite customer, though, if I tried, I bet!

Back to the question at hand: Why would we want to improve or increase our conscious contact with God? We've been on a journey together with Him so far, and on that journey, has He let us down? No, I don't believe so. He has proven faithful to His Word. His guidance thus far seems to be finally leading us to the freedom that we've desired all our lives but haven't been able to reach on our own. So I guess the question could be: Why stop now?

Ever heard the words of someone influential in your life pop into your head when you're faced with a situation? It could've been a coach, a boss, a parent, or an older sibling, perhaps. For me, I often have a former boss's words come up as I'm dealing with someone or a situation. The question pops up: "What would Lynton say or do in this situation?" Then, I take the answer that pops into my head and runs with it because it is usually the best solution. But how do I know what my boss' thoughts or direction would be? Well, I've spent time with him, talked with him, and have walked beside each other as we've faced situations together. Our relationship has been deeper than simply passing on updates like we were Facebook friends. That took time to develop; we worked together for years in a men's recovery program. Now, this is a simplistic example of how our relationship with God benefits us, but I think that you can see how spending time with God serves us. As you get to know Him more, His words and His direction will pop into your head as you face things. You become more and more in tune with His will for your life. You can look back on your experiences over this journey so far and lean on Him for the strength to move forward under His direction. He has proven faithful to do so so far and He will continue to as you move forward. That's what the second part of this step, *"praying only for the knowledge of His will for us and the power to carry that out"* is referring to.

That is the why of this step; we seek to develop our relationship with Him by spending time with Him. It's through His guidance that we've come this far and experienced freedom. Now, to look to the practical side of this, the *how* do we improve our conscious contact with God"? Step 11 says, *"Sought through prayer and meditation"*. We've looked at prayer before. Prayer is nothing more than simply talking to God. It's opening up your heart and sharing with Him your concerns, desires, and love. Prayer doesn't have to be all wrapped up in fancy language and structure. It can be as simple as a cry for "Help!" like we did back in step 3. Prayer is like sitting down to a conversation with someone. You don't use strange formal language when you're getting to know someone, do you? You usually just ask questions and seek out interaction with the other person. Prayer is all about opening up so we can know and be known. Prayer can be asking for things, but we need to keep in mind that God is not a cosmic vending machine. We don't just go to him when we need something, make a request, and He simply dispenses it. We must remember that we're spending time in prayer to get to know Him more. If we remember that He has our best interest at heart, we will be amazed to find ourselves asking for things that He wants for us. Besides, who wants to build a relationship with a vending machine?

So, what do we pray? What does that look like? As I've said before, it can be as simple as having a conversation, and that is what I would suggest. You may feel a bit uncomfortable and don't know where to start. Conversation with someone sitting across a table from you can be hard enough, never mind striking up a conversation with someone you can't even see. For the first while we can even have fears of being one of those crazy people talking to themselves! If you find yourself at a loss for words, don't sweat it. Find a prayer that you like and simply pray it. That could be the Lord's Prayer or the Serenity Prayer to give a couple examples. Now, that may sound a bit contrived. How is that really opening up and sharing our fears and concerns if we're reading a script? Consider when you go to a card shop to buy a card for someone. Do you just grab the first thing you see, or do you read a few, looking for one that speaks what you want to express? Why don't we just write our own card? If you're like me, you don't make a card because you don't really know how to put into words what you want to say. So I go to someone who does have that knack. Using a pre-written prayer, if it lines up with our heart, is no different. I bet over time, you'll find yourself adding to it or substituting your own prayer, just like we end up adding our own little bit of a message in cards we buy and give.

The other part of prayer, and this carries us over into the meditation side of things a bit, is listening. Remember that prayer is a conversation. Conversation, when one-sided, is a bit boring and doesn't really build a relationship. Ever have a conversation with someone who you wonder, when do they breathe? A good piece of wisdom I've heard is that we have two ears and one mouth, and we should use them proportionally. For all the time we spend talking to God, we should take this advice and spend twice as much time listening. I'll admit that's hard, and I struggle to do this myself. We must keep in mind however, that we're looking to Him for guidance, so we need to listen in order for Him to give it.

The second thing this step encourages us to do to connect with God is meditation. What is meditation? Do we need to sit cross-legged, arms outstretched, chanting "ohm"? No, that's not it. Thank goodness because while I might bend to get into that position, unfolding would be another story! Meditation is, in its simplest understanding, consciously choosing to relax and focus our attention on something, in this case, God. So prayer and meditation can very easily go hand in hand. Prayer can be done anywhere, at any time, in the midst of your day and actions. In fact I'd recommend that you make prayer something you find yourself doing all the time. From the time you get up, to standing in line at the bank or sitting at your desk at work, to laying in your bed at night.

Prayer you may find, is particularly special and can take on even more depth and meaning when it is paired with meditation. When we take the time to stop and focus on spending time with God, we begin to have quality time as opposed to quantity time. Now, just like in life, we can't designate that this is going to be "quality time". We can't make an entry in our day timer, "From 4 until 5 today, God and I will spend some quality time". We can help set the stage for it by creating conditions that are conducive to it happening though. How do we "set the stage?" The easiest thing to do is find a quiet, comfortable place - someplace where you won't be disturbed. Jesus told His disciples to get away and go into a closet, closing the door behind them and praying to God in private. This ideally needs to be some alone time with just you and God. That can be in a quiet room, a private beach, a park bench, wherever you find some peace of mind or a refuge. Myself, I like to go down to a local church where they have what they call the "Adoration Chapel". It's a little chapel in the back of the building, open 24 hours a day, where people can go and sit in silence and pray. It's open to everyone, and you don't need to be from that church.

Wherever works for you, find a place and set aside sometime when you won't be disturbed. Don't try to squeeze it in the 15 minutes between appointments. Turn off the cell phone - easier said than done. When you're in that place, close your eyes, take a couple of minutes to pay attention to your breathing, and relax. Then just talk to God, whether you do that out loud or just quietly in your own thoughts. Take time to thank Him for what He's done and is doing in your life. Ask Him for guidance with whatever is on your heart, and then simply sit and listen. Remember the ratio from earlier? 2 ears, 1 mouth. Listen for that still, small voice inside as He testifies to your spirit. As you sit there, you may find that thoughts of what still needs to be done today, your honey do list, or concerns about work, etc, pop into your mind. Gently grab them and acknowledge them, then set them aside to be dealt with later.

Centre yourself on sitting quietly and being open to hearing what God wants to speak to you. There are any number of ways in which He may choose to communicate. You don't have to hear a booming voice from the heavens! He may choose to do so, but I'd say that's the exception rather than the norm. God may choose to speak quietly to you in your thoughts through words, pictures, and impressions. He may bring up memories of things or times with other people/experiences that seem to apply to the day at hand. I find that He usually speaks to me by highlighting things that are close to my heart that line up with His. That's often how I know that I'm on the right track. A word of caution: remember our amazing ability to self-deceive. Whenever you feel led by God, that He is speaking to you, run it through a quick check. Does what He seems to be saying line up with His character? Is it scriptural? Does it serve others, or is it centred on me? This check should quickly help us discern whether He was truly speaking or if our desires were being projected upon Him and save us a lot of heartache. When the time feels like it's right to end, give it one more minute, then wrap up, thanking God for the time spent together. I bet you'll be amazed at the growth in your relationship as you get into the habit of spending time with God in this way.

A heads up. Even when we develop this habit, there will be times when we fall out of it. Life will seem to get busy and we put it off, then put it off again. Eventually, we look back and have a hard time remembering when we last spent time with God. Usually this recognition happens about the same time that life seems to be getting to us. Imagine that! Take heart because God hasn't gone anywhere. He's still right there beside you and wants to talk whenever you do. Just jump back on the wagon and have a reunion!

So, in conclusion, I'd like you to consider this: We eat and drink and breathe to "feed" our bodies. Spending time in prayer and meditation are ways that we "feed" our souls. As we continue on this journey, we need to make sure that we're feeding all of our needs: body and spirit. So, I encourage you to take this step to spend time with God, seeking His will for your life. He has been faithful to bring you this far, and He's not going to abandon you now. You will be surprised as you find yourself seeking His will that your prayers will become more focused on others. It will soon become second nature to seek ways to serve those around you.

That shouldn't really surprise us, though. This journey leads us to be made more and more into the image of the ultimate servant, Jesus, as we were originally designed to be. There are some example prayers in the Appendix at the back of this book for you to use if you want as you seek to grow in your relationship with God. Enjoy the journey!

Prayer

Heavenly Father, thank You for wanting to and being available to talk anytime. Give us the courage to step out of our comfort zone and seek You out, to spend time with You. Help us to pour out our hearts and give us ears to hear from You. Thank You, Jesus. Amen.

Questions

1. Am I ready to work on my relationship with God? To seek out His will for my life and step into it? Do I believe that He wants to talk?

2. Set aside some time to engage in this step. Be proactive, relax, and quiet your body and mind. Tell Him what's on your heart, and then stop and listen for His response. What is He saying to you? (Feel free to use one of the prayers at the end of the book)

3. Sometimes He answers right away, sometimes not. Sometimes an answer is "Yes", sometimes "No," and sometimes "Not yet". Based on how He's walked with me so far, am I ready to commit to continuing to build my relationship with Him? To let Him guide me?

Chapter 12
Sleepwalking in Traffic

Here you are...you've made it! The last step of the journey. Hallelujah! We've been looking at the story of the prodigal son, mining it to see what God has to tell us about this journey of restoration. It's had a lot to say. Whenever we pick up His Word, He has something more for us. Don't think that we've exhausted how this particular story can speak to us; remember, it's the *living Word!*

A little disclaimer before we get started. This is the last step we're going to be exploring on this journey. However, the truth of the matter is that the journey doesn't actually end here. As we discussed before, the last three steps, 10, 11 and 12, are referred to as the maintenance steps. We continually cycle through them, striving to continue learning and addressing life on life's terms so that we can continue to grow. We seek to be restored more and more to the life God originally designed for us. By putting into practise what He's taught and walked with us through this journey, we can continue to move forward in our lives. It will fuel within us a sense of hope and security that we will never have to face this road alone, no matter what life throws at us. And that, my friend, is exciting!

So, let's hit the road, so to speak, and explore this last step - step 12.

"Having had a spiritual awakening as a result of these steps, we tried to carry this message to others and to practice these principles in all our affairs."

God's Kingdom is an upside-down Kingdom. In this new way of living, if we want to keep something, we need to give it away, and that's what this step is all about. Makes sense, right? *Not!* That's alright; we'll explore this more in a bit and make some sense of it.

First, we need to look back at where we've come from in order to be able to understand the importance of this current step. Can you think of one word that sums up step 1? What recognition did we come to that got us started on this journey in the first place? One word. *Powerless.* We'd come to the end of our proverbial rope, right? We recognized that, like Paul, left to our own devices, we end up doing what we don't want to do and not doing what we really want to do.

What was the next step we took? What's a one-word summary? *Belief.* So, our second step naturally flowed out of the first. We recognize that we can't do it, so we come to believe that the solution needs to come from outside us. We believe that there is a God who can and wants to lead us to sanity, right?

What came next on our journey? What was the third step in one word? *Decide.* It's very important for us to break down this journey into its simplest terms. One word summaries for each of these steps enable us to hang on to the simplest definitions if we're going to have success. In our human condition, it's way too easy to overanalyze stuff, and we get overwhelmed by the details. Or is that just my experience? Didn't think so. Step 3 - *Decide.* We decided that if we couldn't do it ourselves and there was a God who wanted to help us, we would put ourselves in His care. We'd allow Him to guide us and give us the strength to do things differently.

Step 4 in one word? *Inventory.* Ohhh, that was a hard one, remember? We had to stop running and actually look in the mirror. We needed to get a real understanding of who we are, what we've done and how our choices in life have impacted us and those around us. We took an inventory of our lives and needed to really lean into God in order to be fearless and face the music. Did you really enjoy that step? Not so much, but it was necessary if we were going to continue on this journey.

So, what was step 5? *Confess.* We thought step 4 was hard. In this step, we needed to actually go through our inventory and confess to God, to ourselves and to another person how our journey under our own power had gone. That was a pretty daunting task, but when you came out the other side of it, the feeling of freedom from your secrets was pretty amazing, wasn't it? Being actually known and accepted for who and what we are is critically important in our lives. We're communal beings, and it's built into our DNA to be a part of something bigger. Secrets hold the power to break that design and keep us isolated. That's why the restoration into the community that we experience in step 5 is so important if we're going to chart a new course in life.

Halfway there! What was step 6? *Ready.* Ready for what? Having identified and confessed our issues in the past two steps, we were now truly ready to have God remove our defects of character. Step 6 is a bit of a watershed moment where we turn and face a new direction. You're ready to embark on this new journey, to put the past behind you and step into this new life that God has for you.

Step 7 is the practical follow-up to step 6, where we put step 6 into action. What was step 7 – one word? *Remove.* So now we move from being ready to actually walking in new life, asking God to remove our defects of character. How does He remove them? Some He gives us instant freedom from. Others and this is the hard part of walking this new life out; He allows us to experience opportunities to try new ways in His strength and learn new habits. Through time and experience, you get to journey and grow into what He originally designed for you. That's both a daunting and an exciting journey!

The next step, step 8, was? *Willing.* This step is about owning our part in the community. In step 8, we're called to make another list - a list of all the people our actions or inactions perhaps have harmed. This exercise isn't just about putting pen to paper, however. It's about our willingness to truly be a part of community life. We must be willing to try to restore some of what our actions have damaged.

What was step 9 in one word? *Amends.* Step 9 is where the rubber meets the road of step 8. This is about the restoration of relationships and also teaches us about our own limits and responsibilities when it comes to the task. In step 8, we were called to make a list. In step 9, we took that list and tried to make amends where we could. Making amends is really about trying to repair some of the damage to the community that our life prior to this journey caused. This step also teaches us to recognize what's actually in our power and what we need to leave in God's hands. We're called to make amends except where doing so would cause harm to that person or others. In those cases, we're to leave it in God's hands, knowing that He has a plan and that we are not God.

What's the heart behind Step 10? *Checkup.* Step 10 was the beginning of the "maintenance" steps. The step we're going to be looking at in this chapter, step 12, is the last step in that maintenance cycle. Like getting a routine checkup with a doctor in order to stay on top of our game physically, step 10 is where we do a daily check-up on our walk. How did we do today? Did we do the right things, make the right choices, say the right things? If so, we celebrate them and thank God for the strength to continue doing them yet another day. If, in our daily checkup we discover things that we could've handled better, we don't beat ourselves up. We simply look to see if we can do something to set things right and again lean on God for the strength to do better next time. We need to remember that success is found in lifelong learning; we never "arrive." We simply take another step and hopefully learn from the ones that came before.

Lastly, we looked at step 11. What's the one word summary for that step? *Connection.* Step 11 is about our source of strength and guidance to keep walking this path, isn't it? In this step we're to make a point of developing our conscious contact with God. We must continue to seek directions for our next footsteps. Remember, early on, in step 1, we recognized that when we operate in our own strength, things don't go as we hope. So step 11 is really all about continually looking to God to guide us and give us the strength to make the right choices. We can do that through a number of ways but primarily through prayer and meditation. We need to make a point of setting aside time to spend with God and talking with Him. That's how any relationship grows.

So that's the road we've been travelling, which has led us to where we are today, step 12. As I indicated earlier...you've made it! We're on the last step of the journey we've been on. Hallelujah! What was step 12 again?

"Having had a spiritual awakening as a result of these steps, we tried to carry this message to others and to practice these principles in all our affairs."

Now, we can get back to what I said before about God's Kingdom being an upside-down Kingdom. In this new way of living, if we want to keep something, we need to give it away, and that's what this step is all about.

Let's look first at the beginning of this step - *"having had a spiritual awakening."* What exactly is that talking about? Well, that was part of the reason I wanted to review our journey so far. It's by looking back that we can gain some clarity on where we've come from, what we've done, how it was done and who was responsible. When we think back to life *before* we chose this path, we were lost weren't we? In essence, we were stumbling around blindly, trying to get somewhere. But without any actual idea what "somewhere" looked like, never mind how to get there! It was only by engaging in these steps and following the course laid out in them that we came to see what life can and is meant to look like. Awareness opens the doors of choice. Instead of blindly stumbling in the dark, now we have a light shining at our feet, illuminating the path and guiding us forward. We're actually getting somewhere these days!

Would you agree that this journey so far could be looked at in terms of having an awakening? Like we were sleepwalking before, not really conscious of where we were going, what we were doing, perhaps even putting ourselves in danger. Ever sleepwalked before? It could be pretty dangerous if you left your house and walked out into traffic! That's essentially what we were doing: sleepwalking in traffic. We were barely getting missed by speeding cars, probably even getting brushed occasionally. Then someone honked at us and awoke us to realize where we were. We realized that we needed to get back safely onto the sidewalk, off the street, back where pedestrians are supposed to be and out of where vehicles are meant to travel. The "sidewalk," or path for us today, is where we're striving to stay.

Guess what? If we turn to look back at the street, what do we see? The street is crowded with sleepwalkers! In fact, there seems to be more of them than cars! Now, we need to explore the story of the prodigal son again to see what it has to share with us about this step. Can you remember where to find the story of the prodigal son? Lk 15:11-31. The prodigal son we know "woke up" in the street of a far-off land and made his way back to the sidewalk to home. His father, like our Heavenly Father, restored him and helped him to get back on the right path. They even threw a celebration party. Now, that's a lot of honking to keep him awake and conscious of what had been given to him!

In the story, though, the father turns and looks back out into the street and sees that his other son, too, is a victim of sleepwalking. He has strayed out into the street and continues to make decisions keeping him there. Decisions that break down the community and relationships when he doesn't join in and welcome his brother home. So, what does the father do? He goes out into the street where his son is and shares with him the good news of his brother's return. He tries to help his son see what has happened and appreciate it for what it is - a life restored! In the story we read that the brother doesn't respond as his father hopes. We do get to see the father living out step 12, however. In Kingdom style, the father gives up the safety of the sidewalk and ventures out into the street to try and reach his son. He walks the talk. He makes himself vulnerable and tries to serve another in the hopes that what he shares helps guide another back onto the path.

So how do we, like the prodigal son's father, walk this step in our own lives? How do we reach the sleepwalkers on the street and help them find the sidewalk? If we were to choose one word to summarize step 12 as we've done for the others, what would it be? *Share.* We need to share what we've found. This step calls us to carry the message to others. Is it really any surprise when we think about it? This step is meant to build on the restoration in our own lives to spread that restoration to others.

What is God's desire for His creation? Peter, writing in his second letter to us, says:

"The Lord is not slow in keeping his promise, as some understand slowness. Instead, he is patient with you, not wanting anyone to perish, but everyone to come to repentance." ~ 2 Peter 3:9 NIV

It's God's desire that none should perish. What was the command Jesus left us with right before He returned to His Father?

"Therefore, go and make disciples of all the nations, baptizing them in the name of the Father and the Son and the Holy Spirit. Teach these new disciples to obey all the commands I have given you. And be sure of this: I am with you always, even to the end of the age." ~ Mt 28:19-20 NLT

Go and make disciples of all the nations - to reach those who are lost and restore them to the design that God set in motion from the beginning! We have the light shining at our feet, lighting the way forward. It's now our job to invite others to come and walk in this light as well. We do that by simply sharing our stories and our own journey experiences. Contrary to what you may think, each and every one of us has a story worth sharing. Our journeys have value because it's through them that God wants to not only speak to us but also to others.

So does that mean we should carry Gospel tracts or pamphlets with us? We should approach people on the street, in restaurants, at bus stops, the mall, with a Bible open and try to explain God's love for them. That could be the case, sometimes those are the things, the ways God will use to touch someone, to honk and awaken them. Those can all be valid ways, so we can't simply discount them and write them off wholeheartedly. However, if we look at the second half of this step, we will find the way that God uses us most of the time to impact and reach those around us. *"Practise these principles in all our affairs"* - that sounds like walking the talk to me, how about you? Or perhaps another way of saying it is "practicing what we preach". When someone practices what they preach, or their walk matches their talk, what does that say? What message does that send? I'd say that it shows that what they say actually has some truth to it, that it has validity. Sharing something with someone works best when they trust us and what we're saying.

So if we walk the path set before us faithfully, trusting and leaning on God as our experience has taught us to do, what's the message we're carrying? A message of hope in another way. A message that there *is another way*. That there is a map, and that sleepwalkers can awake and find their way back onto the sidewalk where life is meant to be walked.

Remember a moment ago, I said that tracts and approaching people with the truth of God's Word shouldn't be discounted, that God can use them? How about we just reverse the order of this step? Let's put the horse back in front of the cart. The horse is us walking to the best of our ability in the newly restored life we've discovered. The cart is what we're hauling with us - our story of the journey so far. So maybe instead of a tract, a pamphlet with a set of directions of how to know Jesus, how about we take some time to consider our story? How can I best share what God has done in my life? What are some specific examples of what and how God has moved in my experience? How did I get to know Him? What does my roadmap look like that has gotten me here? Once we have taken the time to consider these things, we need to be ready to step into those conversations when they come up boldly. People will see our lives, how we live them, and the changes we've undergone and want to know *what happened.* We need to be ready to answer those questions - to *carry this message to others*. That's how God wants to use us - that's His plan for restoration. Jesus left us with this command - go into the world and make disciples!

The sidewalk metaphor is exactly that: a metaphor for the path of safety, where we're meant to walk, where God designed us to be. Life is not meant to be lived on the sidelines; however, we follow a God who is too concerned with us to stay on a bus bench. We're called to venture into the street as well, where the action is. The only way we can do that effectively is as the horse, putting one foot faithfully in front of the other. We're harnessed to our story and ready to take on passengers so they can meet God for themselves.

That's what step 12 is and, frankly, *what life's all about!* So, are you ready to continue walking? Honk your horn and awaken others to the journey!

Prayer

Heavenly Father, thank You for honking and waking us up. Thank you for guiding us back to safety. Now as we enter traffic, keep us safe and help us to awaken others to the life You've always planned for them. Thank You, Jesus. Amen.

Questions

1.As I look back at this journey, these steps have led me to where I am today, where do I see God's fingerprints the most? Take time to consider how you would tell your story if someone were to ask.

2.When I look around me, who do I see that is in need of waking up? How can I "honk my horn" with my life and share with them the roadmap I've found?

3.What have these last three steps taught me about staying on this new path? Am I ready to commit to walking them regularly, daily even, in order to continue moving forward and walking in His plan for my life?

Epilogue

I indicated at the beginning of this book that we need to remember that the 12 steps were not created by the "A" community. They're simply Biblical principles that have been written down in understandable language by people gifted to do so. As such, they are meant for *everyone;* they are a life-changing path for all to follow. It is my hope that this text has highlighted that reality. May it serve as a tool in our belts, equipping us to grow and engage in life regardless of our background.

Over the years, as this has been on my heart, this message has taken a number of formats to serve the situation I found myself in. Whether that was sharing a principle in a meeting over coffee or through a message series, these truths have always allowed me to grow and point to Jesus. This present form, the book in your hands, is not truly my creation. I just get to be the one who shares the message again and points to God, who makes all things possible. Thank You, Father, for the honour to serve and may Your Name be lifted high!

Hopefully, you've enjoyed this journey. I know I have. I hope and pray that it has served you well and that you're living in the restoration that our Heavenly Father desires for us. I pray that we all will stay harnessed to our Father, excited to see where He guides us next and who He has joined us on the journey! Now, I wouldn't be much of a pastor if we didn't end with a benediction, would I?

May The Lord bless you and keep you; may The Lord make His face shine on you and be gracious to you; may The Lord turn His face toward you and give you peace. God bless, and I'll see you on the road for the next part of the journey!

your brother in Christ,

Brad

Endnotes

1. AA
2. http://dictionary.cambridge.org/dictionary/english/believe
3. Louis Giglio, Global Leadership Summit, 2015
4. http://www.aa.org/assets/en_US/en_step9.pdf
5. http://www.aa.org/assets/en_US/en_step9.pdf

References

The Twelve Steps of Alcoholics Anonymous,. Retrieved March 17, 2017 from http://www.aa.org/assets/en_US/smf-121_en.pdf

Prayer of St. Francis,. Retrieved March 17, 2017 from http://recoverytimes.com/stfrancis.html

Holy Bible, New International Version, Bible Gateway. Retrieved March 17, 2017 from https://www.biblegateway.com/passage/?search=Lk+15%3A11-31&version=NIV

Holy Bible, New Living Translation, Bible Gateway. Retrieved March 17, 2017 from https://www.biblegateway.com/passage/?search=Lk+15%3A11-31&version=NLT

Holy Bible, King James Version, Bible Gateway. Retrieved March 17, 2017 from https://www.biblegateway.com/passage/?search=Lk+15%3A11-31&version=KJV

Holy Bible, King James Version, Bible Gateway. Retrieved March

17, 2017 from

https://www.biblegateway.com/passage/?search=Lk+15%3A11-31&version=MSG

Appendix 1
Salvation Prayer

Heavenly Father, thank you for today. Thank you for loving me - a sinner and refusing to turn Your back on me. Thank You for loving me so much, Jesus, that You would die for me on a cross. I am sorry for walking my own way, and I ask for Your forgiveness. Please help me to walk with You today, tomorrow and evermore. In Your name, I pray, Jesus. Amen.

Appendix 2
Sample Prayers

Lord's Prayer

Our Father who art in Heaven,

Hallowed be thy name;

Thy kingdom come; Thy will be done

On earth as it is in heaven.

Give us this day our daily bread;

And forgive us our trespasses

As we forgive those who trespass against us;

And lead us not into temptation,

But deliver us from evil.

For thine is the kingdom

And the power And the glory,

Forever and ever.Amen.

Serenity Prayer

God grant me the SERENITY to accept the things I cannot change;

COURAGE to change the things I can;

and WISDOM to know the difference.

Living one day at a time, enjoying one moment at a time;

accepting hardships as the pathway to peace;

taking, as He did, this sinful world as it is, not as I would have it:

Trusting that He will make all things right if I surrender to His Will;

that I may be reasonably happy in this life

and supremely happy with Him forever in the next. Amen

From Twelve Steps and Twelve Traditions

Lord, make me a channel of thy peace—that where there is hatred, I may bring love—that where there is wrong, I may bring the spirit of forgiveness—that where there is discord, I may bring harmony—that where there is error, I may bring truth—that where there is doubt, I may bring faith—that where there is despair, I may bring hope—that where there are shadows, I may bring light— that where there is sadness, I may bring joy. Lord, grant that I may seek rather comfort than to be comforted— to understand than to be understood—to love than to be loved. For it is by self-forgetting that one finds. It is by forgiving that one is forgiven. It is by dying that one awakens to Eternal Life. Amen."

http://recoverytimes.com/stfrancis.html

Appendix 3

12 Steps Overview

Step 1 - Powerless

Step 2 - Belief

Step 3 - Decide

Step 4 - Inventory

Step 5 - Confess

Step 6 - Ready

Step 7 - Remove

Step 8 - Willing

Step 9 - Amends

Step 10 - Check-up

Step 11 - Contact

Step 12 - Share

Appendix 4
12 Steps of Alcoholics Anonymous

1. We admitted we were powerless over alcohol—that our lives had become unmanageable.
2. Came to believe that a Power greater than ourselves could restore us to sanity.
3. Made a decision to turn our will and our lives over to the care of God *as we understood Him.*
4. Made a searching and fearless moral inventory of ourselves.
5. Admitted to God, to ourselves, and to another human being, the exact nature of our wrongs.
6. Were entirely ready to have God remove all these defects of character.
7. Humbly asked Him to remove our shortcomings.
8. Made a list of all persons we had harmed, and became willing to make amends to them all.

9. Made direct amends to such people wherever possible, except when to do so would injure them or others.

10. Continued to take personal inventory and, when we were wrong promptly admitted it.

11. Sought through prayer and meditation to improve our conscious contact with God *as we understood Him*, praying only for knowledge of His will for us and the power to carry that out.

12. Having had a spiritual awakening as the result of these steps, we tried to carry this message to alcoholics and to practice these principles in all our affairs.

http://www.aa.org/assets/en_US/smf-121_en.pdf

Appendix 5
7 Deadly Sins

Pride - is excessive belief in one's own abilities that interferes with the individual's recognition of the grace of God. It has been called the sin from which all others arise. Pride is also known as Vanity.

Greed - is the desire for material wealth or gain, ignoring the realm of the spiritual. It is also called Avarice or Covetousness.

Lust - is an inordinate craving for the pleasures of the body.

Anger - is manifested in the individual who spurns love and opts instead for fury. It is also known as Wrath.

Gluttony - is an inordinate desire to consume more than that which one requires.

Envy - is the desire for others' traits, status, abilities, or situation.

Sloth - is the avoidance of physical or spiritual work.

http://www.deadlysins.com/

"Hey Pig, Keep the Slop. I'm Going Home!"

🌐 http://www.bradgamble.com

f https://www.facebook.com/authorbradgamble

📷 https://www.instagram.com/authorbradgamble/